aki BOOK FARE

# FROM THE EARTH TO THE MOON

## JULES VERNE

**AIRMONT**

AIRMONT PUBLISHING COMPANY, INC.
22 EAST 60TH STREET · NEW YORK 10022

**An Airmont Classic**
*specially selected for the Airmont Library*
*from the immortal literature of the world*

THE SPECIAL CONTENTS OF THIS EDITION
© Copyright, 1967, by
Airmont Publishing Company, Inc.

ISBN: 0-8049-0142-2   FROM THE EARTH TO THE MOON

# FROM THE EARTH TO THE MOON

## JULES VERNE

### Introduction

Many people believe that a special Providence guides the person with outstanding talent and capabilities into the particular areas where these talents will be expressed to their highest possible effect; and this Providence often operates by closing all other avenues of expression, sometimes abruptly slamming doors in the subject's face. The career of Jules Verne, born at Nantes on February 8, 1828, certainly substantiates such belief.

Some authors have virtually lived and breathed writing, some composers lived and breathed music, from the cradle, but such was not the case with young Jules. His first great desire was to travel; he and his younger brother, Paul, haunted the docks by day and read travel books by candlelight when they should have been sleeping. And when they were unable to read, they would invent stories of travels to tell each other.

Paul became a traveler at the age of eighteen, when he joined the Navy, but there was no such fulfillment in sight for Jules. He had tried to stow away on a schooner bound for the West Indies, but thanks to scientific invention, to which he would become so devoted later on, he was discovered and brought back. Young Jules returned unwillingly to school, not yet dreaming that the talent he had shown in telling travel tales to Paul meant anything beyond momentary amusement and escape from frustration.

The first sign of a vocation came to Jules when he discovered

3

the romantic poets who wrote for the theater; in those days, most plays were still written in poetry, and this discovery turned Jules's imagination away from travel to distant lands. Now he decided he wanted to live in Paris and write plays for the theater; he started at once to work on plays and poems in his spare time.

Needless to say, this was not the career that M. Pierre Verne envisioned for his elder son. It was assumed that the first son of a successful lawyer would follow in his father's footsteps, so when Paul went off to the Navy, Jules was sent to the Sorbonne in Paris to study law.

The Sorbonne was not like colleges and universities in America, or England, where the student was checked carefully on the matter of class attendance, parents notified if this seemed to be deficient, and the student expelled if he cut too many classes. Tuition fees were paid, and eventually the student was expected to present himself for examinations, to determine whether he received a degree or not. What happened in between was entirely up to the young man.

Once in Paris, Jules lost no time in taking advantage of the great opportunities open to him, as he saw them. He submitted a verse drama he had written in Nantes to one of the theaters, hobnobbed with acquaintances from the studios in the Latin Quarter, and learned painfully that one had to have connections in order to make an entrance into this world. In the months that passed, he learned how easy it is for a young man living on an allowance from home to go into debt. One can picture the feelings of Pierre Verne when he paid an unexpected visit to his son after a number of months and found that Jules had not attended a single class at the Sorbonne. The boy asserted his independence and his plea was granted: he could pursue his chimerical career as he chose—and since he was independent, there would be no further subsidy from home!

A chance encounter with Alexandre Dumas resulted in the great man's friendship, a little assistance, and some excellent advice. If you want to become a writer, Dumas told young Verne, then you must write, write, write every day at a given time. Don't sit around and wait for inspiration; take your pen in hand and write what comes to you then and there. If you have talent, this will result in inspiration coming to you.

There were some very minor successes, by way of collaborations on operetta librettos, and the day came when Verne laid down his pen in momentary despair at the realization that he really wasn't interested in writing the sort of material that would sell to the theaters. It was during this period of discouragement that the next door was shown to him—a seemingly strange door, the door of the public libraries.

Here he found the awakening of his earlier dreams of travel as he pored over books, finding in the course of inveterate reading that he had a marvelously retentive memory. And here he found an even greater source of wonder and inspiration than travelogues in the natural sciences. The public libraries became Jules Verne's alma mater, and he would graduate from this school *summa cum laude*.

Somewhere in this period, he came upon the tales of Edgar Allan Poe, translated by the greatest poet of the times, Charles Baudelaire. It has been truly said that the author can choose his own parents, and Verne chose Poe for his literary father. It was the logic, the precision, the scrupulous attention to detail in Poe's stories, as well as the breadth of imagination, that fascinated the young Frenchman. Other elements in the great American author were less attractive to him: Poe, the author of weird and "supernatural" fiction, was a materialist; not only that, Poe went so far as to distort and invent science in order to lock out any suggestion of religious truth. This did not set well with Verne, who was a religious man all his life; yet, oddly enough, there is no trace of his Catholic viewpoint in his best-known fiction.

Eventually, he had to admit what seemed at the time as defeat to his writing ambitions. Dreamer though he was, there was a hard core of practicality in Verne; he would pursue a vision just so far; he could not continue to live in vague hopes and poverty.

The solution would seem to us in the present world a wildly romantic one—he would marry a rich woman. But in Paris at the time, this was far from an impractical goal. Yet, the romantic element had its inning; Verne actually fell in love with a twenty-six-year-old widow whom he met at a friend's marriage feast, wooed her in a whirlwind campaign which resulted in an engagement within a week—and then learned that his Honorine had 50,000 francs to bring to the oncoming marriage! Pierre Verne added a substantial sum of money to his heartfelt blessings, but that good lawyer knew better than to withhold a string. Jules would now become respectable; he would take a position in a stockbroker's office, in which his father would buy him an interest.

Jules Verne now had a loving wife, a respectable position, and financial security. No more hobnobbing with Bohemians, no more days in the public library, no more connections with the theater— now he had become a man and must put away childish things.

Then came the meeting with Felix Tourachon (Nadar), and

his scheme for making an airborne voyage over Europe in a greatly improved balloon. Life suddenly became interesting and wonderful again for Jules as he entered wholeheartedly into Nadar's scheme, drew upon his imagination and scientific background to help design the improvements needed, and secretly made plans to accompany Nadar in the flight.

But when the time came for the flight, a crisis at the Stock Exchange demanded that Verne stick to his post. There was only one escape from this intolerable disappointment; he sat down and began to write about an imaginary journey in a balloon, inventing on paper innumerable improvements that had not appeared in the actual *Gigant*. (Nadar's balloon voyage was a failure, after all.) This imaginary journey did not take place over Europe, but over Africa. Verne's retentive memory gave him the ability to describe such a voyage as well, perhaps better, than any explorer who had been to Africa. He called the novel *Five Weeks in a Balloon*, and he sent it to the publisher, Jules Hetzel.

If there is a special roll of honor in heaven for those editors who guided promising authors, Hetzel's name stands high upon it. He gave the manuscript of Verne's first novel back to him, told him exactly what the story needed, and urged him to leave the Stock Exchange and come to write for him. He offered 20,000 gold francs for two novels a year, a series of "extraordinary journeys," and went over the expansion and revision of *Five Weeks in a Balloon* until both he and the still-incredulous author were completely satisfied.

The first edition of the book went on sale January 1, 1863; by the end of the week, it was sold out. Now, said Hetzel, what will you write for me next?

The answer astounded him. His new author had already decided that the next story would be about a journey to the moon! Unlike the numerous fanciful tales of such voyages which had appeared in the past, this story would be written in accordance with the latest scientific discoveries.

This was 1863; the Civil War was still raging in the United States and it was as yet by no means certain that the Confederate States could not gain their independence from the Federal Union. Verne places his story in a United States where the war is over and the Union has been preserved; but we can note from his descriptions of the South (the great moon-shot is made in Florida) that the terrible devastation of Sherman's march to the sea, and the bitterness it caused, has not yet taken place.

During the war, a unique society is formed in Baltimore—the Gun Club—the sole requirement for membership being that the applicant must have invented a cannon, or at least improved upon a cannon, or invented or improved upon some other firearm. The membership spreads all over the country, and as the war continues, enthusiasm grows.

Then the war comes to an end—a black day for the members of the Gun Club. What future is there for its unique services to the military arts? The club's President, Impy Barbicane, calls a special meeting, assuring members that there will be an announcement of the greatest importance. He lays before them a proposal which takes their collective breath away: the Gun Club will sponsor a monster cannon which will fire a projectile to the moon! Barbicane cites a battery of facts and figures about Earth's satellite and about cannons, projectiles, and ballistics, to convince them that this stupendous feat is actually possible.

The whole world watches, and the nations contribute to the funds, while Barbicane, J. T. Maston, and others proceed with their tremendous project. But even Barbicane and Maston find themselves breathless when they receive a telegram from the great French explorer, Michel Ardan: "Substitute for your spherical shell a cylindro-projectile. I shall go inside it. . . ."

*From the Earth to the Moon* was the first story of a moon-flight using the rocket principle. It was a tremendous success, and the public waited breathlessly for the sequel, *Round the Moon*, wherein the space journey is described in detail.

We know today, of course, that a projectile fired from a cannon is not a feasible spaceship, but were there grounds for considering the story impossible in 1863?* Actually, there were, and Verne was aware of them. He presents the facts in such a manner as to tip off the reader who might otherwise have been misled, but not in such a way as to spoil the illusion. Captain Nicholl presents the scientific objections correctly in the story; but for the sake of the story, these are argued down, and things come out as the members of the Gun Club believe they will.

These first two novels were immediate successes, and now the path was clear; it was as if the many diverse threads in Verne's career had been gathered together—the desire to travel, the ambition to write, the fascination in reading of strange lands and natural science, the attraction of the theater—into a single pattern. Jules Verne had been guided to the right places and to the right people at the right times. His willingness to work hard,

* Heretofore, I have seen the date for *From the Earth to the Moon* listed as 1865, following rather than preceding *A Journey to the Center of the Earth*. Franz Born contends that the moon story was written in 1863 in his *Jules Verne: The Man Who Invented the Future*, and the internal evidence cited above makes this believable. RAWL

his excellent memory, and his never-still imagination were his own contribution.

Now the days of frustration in his ambitions were over, and the series of imaginary voyages grew like an avalanche. *A Journey to the Center of the Earth* (Airmont 1963) is unique in that it is the only well-known story of Verne's where the author has deliberately turned his back upon scientific plausibility and written without reservations, as we find in *From the Earth to the Moon*, of the impossible. Perhaps he was fascinated by the "hollow Earth" hypotheses that were current at the time; in any event, he saw the notion as an inspiration for a wonderful adventure, and once given the fundamental impossibility, Verne proceeds in the best manner of the accomplished science-fiction author, working out each detail logically. *Twenty Thousand Leagues Under the Sea* (1869—Airmont, 1963) ranks highest among the well-known novels for its wealth of projected improvements to the submarine; and in some respects, the original *Nautilus* is still in advance of today's atomic-powered namesake.

A trip to the United States gave Verne a firsthand background for many of the details in *Robur, the Conqueror*, which he wrote in 1886. Verne foresaw the contest to come between the heavier-than-air and the lighter-than-air flying machine; he examined the advantages and disadvantages of each in detail and predicted that the heavier-than-air machine would prove to be superior. And Robur's *Albatross* employs both the helicopter and the forward propeller; there would be years of experiment, and seeming superiority of the dirigible, before the world was convinced that Jules Verne had given the right answer nearly twenty years before the first heavier-than-air flight.

Verne's greatest success, in fact, one of the most successful novels of the entire nineteenth century, was a story which could be called science fiction only by stretching the term—and the term did not exist in those days. Cooks Tours offered a trip around the world in ninety days. Jules Verne examined the resources available for rapid travel in the 1870's and came to the conclusion that ten days could be lopped off that figure. He put his argument into the mouth of the imperturbable Phileas Fogg, and the famous wager was made. (That such a story's being outdated does not harm it was proved some years ago when Michael Todd's splendid film version was released—the most faithful presentation of a Verne story to go before the cameras.)

Like his younger contemporary, H. G. Wells, Jules Verne wrote with the nineteenth century's faith in science as a liberator and the key to a sane and happy world where ignorance, vice, poverty, disease, and the stupendous folly of war would become things of a forgotten past. And like Wells, Jules Verne came to realize that this faith was a chimera; although he died nearly a decade before the Great War shattered Wells's visions, Verne had realized that science alone is no answer to the human condition.

His later novels show his increasing bitterness; and one of the best examples of this is the contrast between the character of Robur, who, in *Robur the Conqueror*, is eager to offer his discoveries to the world for mankind's benefit, but who, in *The Master of the World* (Airmont 1965), is no longer willing to share his secrets. He will rule by means of his discoveries, and force peace and decency upon a world all too eager to follow destructive leaders. But where H. G. Wells, turning to the same solution of benevolent tyranny on the part of scientists with tremendously advanced technologies, has such self-appointed saviors succeed, Verne has Robur suffer defeat. Verne had learned the bitter lesson thoroughly, where Wells had not.

Verne died on March 24, 1905, loved and honored the world over.

ROBERT A. W. LOWNDES

# CONTENTS

## CHAPTER 1

# THE GUN CLUB

During the Federal War in the United States, a new and influential club was founded in the city of Baltimore, Maryland. It is common knowledge how rapidly the taste for military matters grew amongst that nation of ship-owners, shopkeepers, and mechanics. Mere tradesmen jumped their counters to become extemporized captains, colonels, and generals, without having ever passed the School of Instruction at West Point: nevertheless, they quickly rivalled their compeers of the old continent, and, like them, carried off victories by dint of lavish expenditure in ammunition, money, and men.

But the point in which the Americans singularly outdistanced the Europeans was in the science of *gunnery*. Not, indeed, that their weapons were better than theirs, but that they exhibited unheard-of dimensions, and consequently attained hitherto unheard-of ranges. In point of grazing, plunging, oblique, or enfilading, or point-blank firing, the English, French, and Prussians have nothing to learn; but their cannon, howitzers, and mortars are mere pocket-pistols compared with the formidable engines of the American artillery.

This fact need surprise no one. The Yankees, the first mechanicians in the world, are engineers—just as the Italians are musicians and the Germans metaphysicians—by right of birth. Nothing is more natural, therefore, than for them to apply their audacious ingenuity to the science of gunnery.

Now when an American has an idea, he at once seeks a second American to share it. If there be three, they elect a president and two secretaries. Given *four*, they name a keeper of records, and the office is ready for work; *five*, they convene a general meeting, and the club is fully constituted. So things were managed in Baltimore. The inventor of a new cannon associated himself with its caster and its borer. Thus was formed the nucleus of the "Gun Club." In a single month after its formation it numbered 1,833 effective and 30,565 corresponding members.

One condition was imposed upon every candidate for admission to have designed or (more or less) perfected a cannon; or, in default of a cannon, at least a fire-arm of some description. It may, however, be mentioned that mere inventions of revolvers, five-shooting carbines, and similar small arms, met with but little consideration. Artillerists always commanded favour.

The estimation in which these gentlemen were held, according to one of the most scientific exponents of the Gun Club, was "proportional to the masses of their guns, and in the direct ratio of the square of the distances attained by their projectiles."

The Gun Club once founded, it is easy to imagine the result of the inventive genius of the Americans. Their military weapons attained colossal proportions, and their projectiles, exceeding the prescribed limits, unfortunately occasionally cut in two some unoffending bystanders. These inventions, in fact, left far in the rear the timid instruments of European artillery.

It is but fair to add that these Yankees, brave as they have ever proved themselves to be, did not confine themselves to theories and formulæ, but that they paid heavily, *in propriâ personâ*, for their inventions. Amongst them were officers of all ranks, from lieutenants to generals; military men of every age, from those who were just making their *début* in the profession of arms up to those who had grown old on the gun-carriage. Many had found their rest on the field of battle whose names figured in the "Book of Honour" of the Gun Club; and of those who made good their return the greater proportion bore the marks of their indisputable valour. Crutches, wooden legs, artificial arms, steel hooks, caoutchouc jaws, silver craniums, platinum noses, were all to be found; and it was calculated by the great statistician Pitcairn that throughout the Gun Club there was not quite one arm between four persons, and exactly two legs between six.

Nevertheless, these valiant artillerists took no particular

account of these little facts, and felt justly proud when the despatches of a battle returned the number of victims at tenfold the quantity of the projectiles expended.

One day, however—sad and melancholy day!—peace was signed between the survivors of the war; the thunder of the guns gradually ceased, the mortars were silent, the howitzers were muzzled for an indefinite period, the cannon, with muzzles depressed, were returned into the arsenal, the shot were repiled, all bloody memories were effaced; the cotton-plants grew luxuriantly in the well-manured fields, all mourning garments were laid aside, together with grief; and the Gun Club was relegated to profound inactivity.

Some few of the more advanced and inveterate theorists set once more to work upon calculations regarding the laws of projectiles. They reverted invariably to gigantic shells and howitzers of unparalleled calibre. Still, in default of practical experience, what was the value of mere theories? Consequently, the club-rooms became deserted, the servants dozed in the ante-chambers, the newspapers grew mouldy on the tables, sounds of snoring came from dark corners, and the members of the Gun Club, erstwhile so noisy in their sessions, were reduced to silence by this disastrous peace and gave themselves up wholly to dreams of a Platonic kind of artillery.

"This is horrible!" said Tom Hunter one evening, while rapidly carbonizing his wooden legs in the fire-place of the smoking-room; "nothing to do! nothing to look forward to! what a loathsome existence! When shall the guns again wake us in the morning with their delightful reports?"

"Those days are gone by," said jolly Bilsby, trying to extend his missing arms. "It used to be delightful! One invented a gun, and hardly was it cast when one hastened to try it in the face of the enemy! Then one returned to camp with a word of encouragement from Sherman or a friendly shake of the hand from M'Clellan. But now the generals are gone back to their counters; and in place of projectiles, they despatch bales of cotton. By jove, the future of gunnery in America is lost!"

"Ay! and no war in prospect!" continued the famous James T. Maston, scratching with his steel hook his gutta-percha cranium. "Not a cloud in the horizon! and that too at such a critical period in the progress of the science of artillery! Yes, gentlemen! I who address you have myself this very morning perfected a model (plan, section, elevation, etc.) of a mortar destined to change all the conditions of warfare!"

"No! is it possible?" replied Tom Hunter, his thoughts reverting involuntarily to a former invention of the Hon. J. T. Maston, by which, at its first trial, he had succeeded in killing three hundred and thirty-seven people.

"Fact!" replied he. "Still, what is the use of so many studies worked out, so many difficulties vanquished? It's mere waste of time! The New World seems to have made up its mind to live in peace; and our bellicose *Tribune* predicts some approaching catastrophes arising out of this scandalous increase of population."

"Nevertheless," replied Colonel Blomsberry, "they are always struggling in Europe to maintain the principle of nationalities."

"Well?"

"Well, there might be some field for enterprise down there; and if they would accept our services——"

"What are you dreaming of?" screamed Bilsby; "work at gunnery for the benefit of foreigners?"

"That would be better than doing nothing here," returned the colonel.

"Quite so," said J. T. Maston; "but still we need not dream of that expedient."

"And why not?" demanded the colonel.

"Because their ideas of progress in the Old World are contrary to our American habits of thought. Those fellows believe that one can't become a general without having served first as an ensign; which is as much as to say that one can't point a gun without having first cast it oneself!"

"Ridiculous!" replied Tom Hunter, whittling with his bowie-knife the arms of his easy chair; "but if that be so there, all that is left for us is to plant tobacco and distil whale-oil."

"What!" roared J. T. Maston, "shan't we spend the rest of our life in perfecting fire-arms? Won't there ever be another chance of trying the ranges of projectiles? Shall the air never again be lighted with the glare of our guns? No international difficulty ever arise to let us declare war against some transatlantic power? Shall not the French sink one of our steamers, or the English, in defiance of the rights of nations, hang a few of our countrymen?"

"No such luck," replied Colonel Blomsberry; "nothing of the kind is likely to happen; and even if it did, we should not profit by it. American susceptibility is fast declining, and we are all going to the dogs."

"It is too true," replied J. T. Maston, with fresh violence; "there are a thousand grounds for fighting, and yet we don't fight. We save up our arms and legs for the benefit of nations who don't know what to do with them! But stop—without going out of one's way to find a cause for war—didn't North America once belong to the English?"

"Undoubtedly," replied Tom Hunter, stamping his crutch with fury.

"Well then," replied J. T. Maston, "why shouldn't England in turn belong to the Americans?"

"It would be but just and fair," returned Colonel Blomsberry.

"Go and propose it to the President of the United States," cried J. T. Maston, "and see how he will receive you."

"Bah!" growled Bilsby between the four teeth which the war had left him; "that will never do!"

"By jove!" cried J. T. Maston, "he mustn't count on my vote at the next election!"

"Nor on ours," all the bellicose invalids replied unanimously.

"Meanwhile," replied J. T. M., "allow me to say that, if I cannot get an opportunity to try my new mortars on a real field of battle, I shall say good-bye to the members of the Gun Club, and go and bury myself in the prairies of Arkansas!"

"And we will accompany you," cried the others.

Matters were in this unfortunate condition, and the club was threatened with approaching dissolution, when an unexpected circumstance occurred to prevent so deplorable a catastrophe.

On the morrow after this conversation every member of

the association received a sealed circular couched in the following terms:


"BALTIMORE, *Oct. 3.*

"The President of the Gun Club has the honour to inform his colleagues that, at the meeting of the 5th instant, he will bring before them a communication of an extremely interesting nature. He requests, therefore, that they will make it convenient to attend in accordance with the present invitation.—Very cordially,

"IMPEY BARBICANE, P.G.C."

## CHAPTER 2

# PRESIDENT BARBICANE'S COMMUNICATION

On the 5th October, at 8 p.m., a dense crowd pressed towards the saloons of the Gun Club at No. 21, Union Square. All the members of the association resident in Baltimore responded to the invitation of their president. As regards the corresponding members, notices were delivered by hundreds throughout the streets of the city, and, large as was the great hall, it was quite inadequate to accommodate the crowd of *savants*. They overflowed into the adjoining rooms, down the narrow passages, into the outer courtyards. There they ran against the vulgar herd who pressed up to the doors, each struggling to reach the front ranks, all eager to learn the nature of the important communication from President Barbicane; all pushing, squeezing, crushing with that perfect freedom of action which is peculiar to the masses when educated in ideas of "self-government."

On that evening a stranger who might have chanced to be in Baltimore could not have gained admission into the great hall for love or money. That was reserved exclusively for resident or corresponding members; no one else could possibly have obtained a place; and the city magnates, municipal councillors, and "select men" were compelled to mingle with the mere townspeople in order to catch stray items of news from the interior.

Nevertheless the vast hall presented a curious spectacle. Its immense area was singularly adapted to its purpose. Lofty pillars formed of cannon, superposed upon huge mortars as a base, supported the fine ironwork of the arches, a perfect piece of cast-iron lacework. Trophies of blunderbuses, matchlocks, arquebuses, carbines, all kinds of firearms, ancient and modern, were picturesquely interlaced against the walls. The gas lit up in full glare myriads of revolvers grouped in the form of lustres, whilst groups of pistols, and candelabra formed of muskets bound together,

completed this magnificent display of brilliance. Models of
cannon, bronze castings, sights covered with dents, plates
battered by the shots of the Gun Club, assortments of ram-
mers and sponges, chaplets of shells, wreaths of projectiles,
garlands of howitzers—in short, all the apparatus of the
artillerist—enchanted the eye by this wonderful arrange-
ment and induced an impression that their real purpose was
ornamental rather than deadly.

At the further end of the saloon the president, assisted by
four secretaries, occupied a large platform. His chair, supported by a carved gun-carriage, was modelled upon the
ponderous proportions of a 32-inch mortar. It was pointed
at an angle of ninety degrees, and suspended upon trun-
nions, so that the president could swing upon it as upon a
rocking-chair, a very agreeable fact in the very hot
weather. Upon the table (a huge iron plate supported upon
six carronades) stood an inkstand of exquisite elegance,
made of a beautifully chased Spanish piece, and a sonnette,
which, when required, could give forth a report equal to that
of a revolver. During violent debates this novel kind of bell
scarcely sufficed to drown the clamour of these excitable
artillerists.

In front of the table benches arranged in zigzag form, like
the circumvallations of a retrenchment, formed a succession
of bastions and curtains set apart for the use of the members of the club; and on this especial evening one might say,
"All the world was on the ramparts." The president was
sufficiently well known, however, for all to be assured that
he would not put his colleagues to discomfort without some
very strong motive.

Impey Barbicane was a man of forty years of age, calm,
cold, austere; of a singularly serious and self-contained de-
meanour, punctual as a chronometer, of imperturbable tem-
per and immovable character, by no means chivalrous, yet
adventurous withal, and always bringing practical ideas to
bear upon the very rashest enterprises; essentially a New-
Englander, a Northern colonist, a descendant of the old
anti-Stuart Roundheads, and the implacable enemy of the
gentlemen of the South, those ancient Cavaliers of the
mother-country. In a word, he was a Yankee to the back-
bone.

Barbicane had made a large fortune as a timber-merchant. Appointed Director of Artillery during the war, he proved fertile in invention. Bold in his conceptions, he contributed powerfully to the progress of that arm and gave an immense impetus to experimental researches.

He was a personage of the middle height, having, by a rare exception in the Gun Club, all his limbs complete. His strongly-marked features seemed drawn by square and rule; and if it be true that, in order to judge of a man's character one must look at his profile, Barbicane, so examined, exhibited the most certain indications of energy, audacity, and sang-froid.

At this moment he was sitting in his arm-chair, silent, absorbed, lost in reflection, sheltered under his high-crowned hat—a kind of black silk cylinder which always seems firmly screwed upon the head of an American.

Just when the deep-toned clock in the great hall struck eight, Barbicane, as if he had been set in motion by a spring, raised himself up. A profound silence ensued, and the speaker, in a somewhat emphatic tone of voice, commenced as follows:

"My brave colleagues, too long already a paralyzing peace has plunged the members of the Gun Club in deplorable inactivity. After a period of years full of incident we have been compelled to abandon our labours, and to stop short on the road of progress. I do not hesitate to state, boldly, that any war which should recall us to arms would be welcome!" (*Cries of "Hear! hear!"*) "But war, gentlemen, is impossible under existing circumstances; and, however we may desire it, many years may elapse before our cannon shall again thunder in the field of battle. We must make up our minds, then, to seek elsewhere some field for the activity which we all pine for."

The meeting felt that the president was now approaching the critical point, and redoubled their attention accordingly.

"For some months past, my brave colleagues," continued Barbicane, "I have been asking myself whether, while confining ourselves to our own particular objects, we could not enter upon some grand experiment worthy of the nineteenth century; and whether the progress of artillery science would not enable us to carry it out to a successful issue. I have been considering, working, calculating; and the result of my studies is the conviction that we are safe to succeed in an enterprise which to any other country would appear wholly impracticable. This project, the result of long elaboration, is the object of my present communication. It is worthy of yourselves, worthy of the antecedents of the Gun Club; and it cannot fail to make some noise in the world."

A thrill of excitement ran through the meeting.

Barbicane, having by a rapid movement firmly fixed his hat upon his head, calmly continued his harangue:

"There is no one among you, my brave colleagues, who has not seen *the Moon*, or, at least heard speak of it. Don't be surprised if I am about to discourse to you regarding this Queen of the Night. It is perhaps reserved for us to become the Columbuses of this unknown world. Only enter into my plans, and second me with all your power, and I will lead you to its conquest, and its name shall be added to those of the thirty-six States which compose this Great Union."

"Three cheers for the Moon!" roared the Gun Club with one voice.

"The moon, gentlemen, has been carefully studied," continued Barbicane, "her mass, density, and weight; her constitution, motions, distance, as well as her place in the solar system, have all been exactly determined. Selenographic charts have been constructed with a perfection which equals, even if it does not surpass, that of our terrestrial maps. Photography has given us proofs of the incomparable beauty of our satellite; in short, all is known regarding the moon which mathematical science, astronomy, geology, and optics can learn about her. But up to the present moment no direct communication has been established with her."

A violent movement of interest and surprise here greeted this remark of the speaker.

"Permit me," he continued, "to recount briefly how certain ardent spirits, starting on imaginary journeys, have penetrated the secrets of our satellite. In the seventeenth century a certain David Fabricius boasted of having seen with his own eyes the inhabitants of the moon. In 1649 a Frenchman, one Jean Baudoin, published a 'Journey performed from the Earth to the Moon by Domingo Gonzalez,' a Spanish Adventurer. At the same period Cyrano de Bergerac published that celebrated 'Journeys in the Moon' which met with such success in France. Somewhat later another Frenchman, named Fontenelle, wrote 'The Plurality of Worlds,' a *chef-d'oeuvre* of its time.

"About 1835 a small treatise, translated from the *New York American*, related how Sir John Herschell, having been despatched to the Cape of Good Hope for the purpose of making some astronomical calculations, had, using a telescope brought to perfection by internal lighting, reduced the apparent distance of the moon to eighty yards! He then distinctly perceived caverns frequented by hippopotami, green mountains bordered by golden lace-work, sheep with horns of ivory, a white species of deer, and inhabitants with membranous wings, like bats. This *brochure*, the work of an American named Locke, had a great sale.

"But, to bring this rapid sketch to a close, I will only add that a certain Hans Pfaal, of Rotterdam, launching himself in a balloon filled with a gas extracted from nitrogen, thirty-seven times lighter than hydrogen, reached the moon after a passage of nineteen hours. This journey, like all the previous ones, was purely imaginary; still, it was the work of a well-known American author—I mean, Edgar Poe!"

"Cheers for Edgar Poe!" roared the assemblage, electrified by their president's words.

"I have now enumerated," said Barbicane, "the experiments which I call purely paper ones, and wholly insufficient to establish serious relations with the Queen of Night. Nevertheless, I am bound to add that some practical geniuses have attempted to establish actual communication with her. Thus, a few years ago, a German geometrician proposed to send a scientific expedition to the steppes of Siberia. There, on those vast plains, they were to describe enormous geometric figures, drawn in characters of reflecting luminosity, amongst which the proposition regarding the 'square of the hypothenuse,' commonly called the *'Ass's bridge'* by the French.

" 'Every intelligent being,' said the geometrician, 'must understand the scientific meaning of that figure. The Selenites, if they exist, will respond by a similar figure; and, a communication being thus once established, it will be easy to form an alphabet which shall enable us to converse with the inhabitants of the moon.' So spoke the German geometrician; but his project was never put into practice, and up to the present day no bond exists between the earth and her satellite. It is reserved for the practical genius of Americans to establish a communication with the sidereal world. The means of arriving thither are simple, easy, certain, infallible—and that is the gist of my present proposal."

A storm of acclamations greeted these words. There was not a single person in the whole audience who was not overcome, carried away, lifted out of himself by the speaker's words!

"Hear! hear! Silence!" resounded from all sides.

As soon as the excitement had partially subsided, Barbicane resumed his speech in a somewhat graver voice.

"You know," said he, "what progress artillery science has made during the last few years, and what a degree of perfection fire-arms of every kind have reached. Moreover, you are well aware that, in general terms, the resisting power of cannon and the expensive force of gunpowder are practically unlimited. Well! starting from this principle, I ask myself whether, supposing sufficient apparatus could be obtained constructed upon the conditions of ascertained resistance, it might not be possible to fire a shot to the moon?"

At these words a mumur of amazement escaped from a thousand panting chests; then succeeded a moment of perfect silence, resembling that profound stillness which precedes the bursting of a thunderstorm. In point of fact, a thunderstorm did peal forth, but it was the thunder of applause, of cries, and of uproar which made the very hall tremble. The president attempted to speak, but could not. It was fully ten minutes before he could make himself heard.

"Suffer me to finish," he calmly continued. "I have looked at the question in all its bearings, I have resolutely attacked it, and by incontrovertible calculations I find that a projectile endowed with an initial velocity of 12,000 yards per second, and aimed at the moon, must necessarily reach it. I have the honour, my brave colleagues, to propose a trial of this little experiment."

# EFFECT OF THE PRESIDENT'S COMMUNICATION

It is impossible to describe the effect produced by the last words of the hon. president—the cries, the shouts, the succession of roars, hurrahs, and all the varied vociferations which the American language is capable of supplying. It was a scene of indescribable confusion and uproar. They shouted, they clapped, they stamped on the floor of the hall. All the weapons in the museum discharged at once could not have more violently set in motion the sound waves. One need not be surprised at this. There are some cannoneers nearly as noisy as their own guns.

Barbicane remained calm in the midst of this enthusiastic clamour; perhaps he wanted to address a few more words to his colleagues, for his gestures demanded silence, and his powerful alarum was worn out by its violent reports. No attention, however, was paid to his request. He was soon torn from his seat and passed from the hands of his faithful colleagues into the arms of a no less excited crowd.

Nothing can astound an American. It has often been asserted that the word "Impossible" is not a French one. People have evidently been deceived by the dictionary. In America, all is easy, all is simple; and as for mechanical difficulties, they are overcome before they arise. Between Barbicane's scheme and its realization no true Yankee would have allowed even the semblance of a difficulty to be possible. A thing with them is no sooner said than done.

The triumphal progress of the president continued throughout the evening. It was a regular torchlight procession. Irish, Germans, French, Scotch, all the heterogeneous units which make up the population of Maryland, shouted in their respective vernaculars; and the "vivas," "hurrahs," and "bravos" were intermingled in inexpressible enthusiasm.

Just at this crisis, as though she comprehended all this

agitation regarding herself, the Moon shone forth with serene splendour, eclipsing by her intense illumination all the surrounding lights. The Yankees all turned their gaze towards her resplendent orb, kissed their hands, called her by all kinds of endearing names. Between eight o'clock and midnight one optician in Jones'-Fall Street made his fortune by the sale of opera-glasses.

Midnight arrived, and the enthusiasm showed no signs of diminution. It spread equally among all classes of citizens —men of science, shopkeepers, merchants, porters, chairmen, as well as "greenhorns," were stirred in their innermost fibres. A national enterprise was at stake. The whole city, high and low, the quays bordering the Patapsco, the ships lying in the basins, disgorged a crowd drunk with joy, gin, and whisky. Everyone chattered, argued, discussed, disputed, applauded, from the gentleman lounging upon the bar-room settee with his tumbler of sherry-cobbler before him down to the waterman who got drunk upon his "knock-me-down" in the dingy taverns of Fell Point.

About 2 a.m., however, the excitement began to subside. President Barbicane reached his house, bruised, crushed, and squeezed almost to a mummy. A Hercules could not have resisted a similar outbreak of enthusiasm. The crowd gradually deserted the squares and streets. The four railways from Ohio, Susquehanna, Philadelphia, and Washington, which converge at Baltimore, whirled away the heterogeneous population to the four corners of the United States, and the city subsided into comparative tranquility.

On the following day, thanks to the telegraph wires, five hundred newspapers and journals, daily, weekly, monthly, or bi-monthly, all took up the question. They examined it under all its different aspects, physical, meteorological, economical, or moral, up to its bearings on politics or civilization. They debated whether the moon had reached its final condition or whether it would undergo any further transformation. Did it resemble the earth when this was destitute of an atmosphere? What kind of spectacle would its hidden hemisphere present? Granting that the question at present was simply that of sending a projectile to the moon, everyone must see that that involved a series of experiments. All must hope that some day America would penetrate the deepest secrets of that mysterious orb; and some even seemed to fear lest its conquest should sensibly derange the equilibrium of Europe.

The project once under discussion, not a single paragraph suggested a doubt of its realization. All the papers, pamphlets, reports—all the journals published by the scientific, literary, and religious societies enlarged upon its advantages; and the Society of Natural History of Boston, the Society of Science and Art of Albany, the Geographical and Statistical Society of New York, the Philosophical Society of Philadelphia, and the Smithsonian of Washington sent innumerable letters of congratulation to the Gun Club, together with offers of immediate assistance and money.

From that day forward Impey Barbicane became one of the greatest citizens of the United States, a kind of Washington of Science. A single trait of feeling, taken from many others, will serve to show the point which this homage of a whole people to a single individual attained.

Some few days after this memorable meeting of the Gun Club, the manager of an English company announced, at the Baltimore theatre, the production of "Much ado about Nothing." But the populace, seeing in that title an allusion damaging to Barbicane's project, broke into the auditorium, smashed the benches, and compelled the unlucky director to alter his playbill. Being a sensible man, he bowed to the public will and replaced the offending comedy by "As you like it;" and for many weeks he realized fabulous profits.

## CHAPTER 4

# REPLY FROM THE OBSERVATORY OF CAMBRIDGE

Barbicane, however, lost not one moment amidst all the enthusiasm of which he had become the object. His first care was to reassemble his colleagues in the board-room of the Gun Club. There, after some discussion, it was agreed to consult the astronomers regarding their part of the enterprise. Their reply once received, they could then discuss the mechanical means, and nothing should be wanting to ensure the success of this great experiment.

A note couched in precise terms, containing a special questionnaire, was then drawn up and addressed to the Observatory of Cambridge in Massachusetts. This city, where the first University of the United States was founded, is justly celebrated for its astronomical staff. There are to be found assembled all the most eminent men of science. Here is to be seen that powerful telescope which enabled Bond to resolve the nebula of Andromeda, and Clarke to discover the satellite of Sirius.* This celebrated institution fully justified on all points the confidence reposed in it by the Gun Club.

So, after two days, the reply so impatiently awaited was placed in the hands of President Barbicane.

It was couched in the following terms:

*"The Director of the Cambridge Observatory to the President of the Gun Club at Baltimore.*

"CAMBRIDGE, *Oct. 7th*
"On the receipt of your favour of the 16th inst., addressed to the Observatory of Cambridge in the name of

* Not a satellite but a small companion star, invisible to unaided sight only because its gleam is swamped by the greater brightness of Sirius. As the "Dog Star's" companion it is sometimes referred to as "the pup."—I.O.E.

the Members of the Baltimore Gun Club, our staff was immediately called together, and it was judged expedient to reply as follows:

"The questions which have been proposed to it are these;

" '1. Is it possible to fire a projectile up to the moon?

" '2. What is the exact distance which separates the earth from its satellite?

" '3. What will be the period of transit of the projectile when given a sufficient initial velocity? and, consequently, at what moment ought it to be fired?

" '4. At what precise moment will the moon be in the most favourable position to be reached by the projectile?

" '5. What point in the heavens ought the cannon to be aimed at?

" '6. What position will the moon occupy at the moment of the projectile's departure?'

"Regarding the *first* question, 'Is it possible to fire a projectile up to the moon?'

"*Answer.*—Yes; provided it possesses an initial velocity of 12,000 yards per second, calculations prove that to be sufficient. In proportion as we recede from the earth the action of gravitation diminishes in the inverse ratio of the square of the distance; that is to say, *at three times a given distance the action is nine times less.* Consequently, the weight of a shot will decrease, and will become reduced to *zero* at the instant that the attraction of the moon exactly counterpoises that of the earth; at 47/52 of its journey. There the projectile will have no weight whatever; and, if it passes that point, it will fall into the moon by the sole effect of the lunar attraction. The *theoretical possibility* of the experiment is therefore absolutely demonstrated; its *success* must depend upon the power of the means employed.

"As to the *second* question. 'What is the exact distance which separates the earth from its satellite?'

"*Answer.*—The moon does not describe a *circle* round the earth, but rather an *ellipse,* of which our earth occupies one of the *foci;* the consequence, is, therefore, that at certain times it approaches nearer to, and at others it recedes farther from, the earth; in astronomical language, it is at one time in *apogee*, at another in *perigee*. Now the difference between its greatest and its least distance is too great to be left out of consideration. In its apogee the moon is 247,552 miles, and in its perigee, only distance 218,657 miles; a fact which makes a difference of 28,895 miles, or more than one ninth of the entire distance. The perigee distance, therefore, ought to serve as the basis of all calculations.

"To the *third* question:

"*Answer.*—If the shot should maintain its initial velocity of 12,000 yards per second, it would require little more than nine hours to reach its destination; but inasmuch as that initial velocity will be continually decreasing, the effect is that, taking everything into consideration, it will occupy 300,000 seconds, 83 hrs. 20 m. in reaching the point where the attraction of the earth and moon will be *in equilibrio*. From this point it will fall into the moon in 50,000 seconds, or 13 hrs. 53 m. 20 sec. It will be desirable, therefore, to discharge it 97 hrs. 13 m. 20 sec. before the arrival of the moon at the point aimed at.

"Regarding question *four*, 'At what precise moment will the moon be in the most favourable position, etc.?'

"*Answer.*—It will be necessary, first of all, to choose the period when the moon will be in perigee, and *also* the moment when she will be crossing the zenith, which will further diminish the entire distance by a length equal to the radius of the earth, i.e. 3,919 miles; the result will be that the distance to be traversed will be 214,976 miles.

"But although the moon passes her perigee every month, she does not always reach the zenith *at exactly the same moment*. She does not appear under these two conditions simultaneously, except at long intervals of time. It will be necessary, therefore, to wait for the moment when her passage in perigee shall coincide with that in the zenith. Now by a fortunate circumstance, on the 4th December in the ensuing year the moon *will* present these two conditions. At midnight she will be in perigee, that is, at her shortest distance from the earth, and at the same moment she will be crossing the zenith.

"On the *fifth* question, 'At what point in the heavens ought the cannon to be aimed?'

"*Answer.*—The preceding remarks being admitted, the cannon ought to be pointed to the zenith of the place. Its fire, therefore, will be perpendicular to the plane of the horizon; and the projectile will most rapidly pass beyond the range of the terrestrial attraction. But, for the moon to reach the zenith of a given place, that place should not exceed in latitude its declination; in other words, it must be within the degrees 0° and 28° of lat. N. or S. In every other spot the fire must necessarily be oblique, which would seriously militate against the success of the experiment.

"As to the *sixth* question, 'What position will the moon occupy in the heavens at the moment of the projectile's departure?'

"*Answer.*—At the moment when the projectile shall be fired into space, the moon, which travels daily forward 13° 10′ 35″, will be distant from the zenith point by four times that quantity, 52° 42′ 20″, a space which corresponds to the path which she will describe during the entire journey of the projectile. But, inasmuch as it is equally necessary to take into account the deviation which the rotary motion of the earth will impart to the shot, and as the shot cannot reach the moon until after a deviation equal to 16 radii of the earth, which, in relation to the moon's orbit, are equal to about eleven degrees, it becomes necessary to add these eleven degrees to those which express the retardation of the moon: in round numbers, about 64 degrees. Consequently at the moment of firing the visual radius the moon will form, with the vertical, an angle of sixty-four degrees.

"These are our answers to the questions proposed to the Observatory of Cambridge by the members of the Gun Club:

"To sum up:

"1st. The cannon ought to be installed in a country situated between 0° and 28° of N. or S. lat.

"2ndly. It ought to be pointed directly towards the zenith.

"3rdly. The projectile ought to be given an initial velocity of 12,000 yds. per second.

"4thly. It ought to be discharged at 10 hrs. 46 m. 40 sec. of the 1st December of the ensuing year.

"5thly. It will meet the moon four days after its discharge, precisely at midnight on the 4th December, at the moment of its transit across the zenith.

"The members of the Gun Club ought, therefore, without delay, to commence the works necessary for such an experiment, and to be prepared to set to work at the moment determined upon; for, if they should suffer this 4th December to go by, they will not find the moon again under the same conditions of perigee and of zenith until eighteen years and eleven days afterwards.

"The Staff of the Cambridge Observatory place themselves entirely at their disposal in respect of all questions of theoretical astronomy; and herewith add their congratulations to those of all the rest of America.

"For the Astronomical Staff,

"J. M. BELFAST,

*"Director of the Observatory of Cambridge."*

## CHAPTER 5

# IGNORANCE AND BELIEF IN THE UNITED STATES

The immediate result of Barbicane's announcement was to publicize all the astronomical facts relative to the Queen of Night. Everybody set to work to study assiduously. One would have thought that the moon had just appeared for the first time, and that no one had ever before caught a glimpse of her in the heavens. The papers revived all the old anecdotes in which the "sun of the wolves" played a part; they recalled the influences which the ignorance of past ages ascribed to her; in short, all America was seized with seleno-mania, or had become moon-mad.

The scientific journals, for their part, dealt more especially with the questions which touched upon the enterprise of the Gun Club. The letter of the Observatory of Cambridge was published by them, and commented upon with unreserved approval.

Until that time most people had been ignorant of how the distance which separates the moon from the earth is calculated. The savants took advantage of this to explain to them that this distance was obtained by measuring the parallax of the moon. The term parallax proving "caviare to the general," they further explained that it meant the angle formed by the inclination of two straight lines drawn from either extremity of the earth's radius to the moon. On doubts being expressed as to the correctness of this method, they immediately proved that not only was the mean distance 234,347 miles, but that the astronomers could not possibly be in error in their estimate by more than 70 miles either way.

To those who were not familiar with the moon's motions, they demonstrated that she possesses two distinct motions, the first being that of rotation upon her axis, the second that of revolution round the earth, accomplishing both alike in an equal period of time, 27⅓ days.

The rotation produces day and night on the surface of the moon; there is only one day and one night in the lunar month, each lasting 354⅓ hours. But, the face turned towards the terrestrial globe is illuminated by it with an intensity equal to the light of fourteen moons. As for the other face, always invisible to us, it has of necessity 354 hours of absolute night, tempered only by that "pale glimmer which falls upon it from the stars."

Some well-intentioned but rather obstinate persons could not at first comprehend how, if the moon invariably turns the same face to the earth during her revolution she can describe one turn round herself. To such was answered, "Go into your dining-room, and walk round the table so as always to keep your face turned towards the centre; by the time you will have achieved one complete round you will have completed one turn round yourself, since your eye will have traversed successively every point of the room. Well, then, the room is the heavens, the table is the earth, and the moon is yourself." And they would go away delighted.

So, then, the moon invariably displays the same face to the earth; to be quite exact, in consequence of certain fluctuations of north and south, and of west and east, termed her libration, she permits rather more than the half, about five-sevenths, to be seen.

As soon as the ignoramuses came to understand as much as the Director of the Observatory himself, they began to get perplexed about the moon's revolution round the earth. At once twenty scientific reviews pointed out that the firmament, with its infinitude of stars, may be considered as one vast dial-plate, upon which the moon travels, indicating the true time to all the inhabitants of the earth. They explained that it is during this movement that the Queen of Night exhibits her different phases; that the moon is *full* when in *opposition* with the sun, when the three bodies are on the same straight line, the earth occupying the centre; that she is *new* when in *conjunction* with the sun, when she is between it and the earth; and lastly, that she is in her *first* or *last* quarter, when she makes with the sun and the earth a right angle with herself at the apex.

Regarding the altitude which the moon attains above the horizon, the letter of the Cambridge Observatory had said all that was to be said in that respect. Everyone knew that this altitude varies according to the latitude of the Observer. But the only zones in which the moon passes the zenith, the point directly over the head of the spectator, are between the twenty-eighth parallels and the equator. Hence the importance of the advice to try the experiment somewhere in that part of the earth so that the projectile might be discharged perpendicularly, and most quickly escape the action of gravitation. This was essential to the success of the enterprise, and continued actively to engage the public attention.

Regarding the path described by the moon in her revolution round the earth, the Cambridge Observatory had demonstrated that this path is a re-entering curve, not a perfect circle, but an ellipse, of which the earth occupies one of the *foci:* it is farthest removed from the earth during its *apogee,* and approaches most nearly to it at its *perigee.*

Such then was the extent of knowledge possessed by every American on the subject, and of which no one could decently profess ignorance. Still, while these principles were being rapidly disseminated, many errors and illusory fears proved less easy to eradicate.

For instance, some worthy persons maintained that the moon was a former comet which, in describing its elongated orbit round the sun, happened to pass near the earth, and became confined within her circle of attraction. These drawing-room astronomers professed to explain the charred aspect of the moon—a disaster which they attributed to the intensity of the solar heat; only, on being reminded that comets have an atmosphere, and that the moon has little or none, they were fairly at a loss for a reply.

Others again, belonging to the genus *funker,* expressed certain fears as to the moon's position. They had heard it said that, according to observations made in the time of the Caliphs, her revolution had become somewhat accelerated. Hence they concluded, logically enough, that an acceleration of motion ought to be accompanied by a corresponding diminution in the distance separating the two bodies; and that, supposing the effect to be continued to infinity, the moon would end by falling into the earth. However, they became reassured as to the fate of future generations on being apprised that, according to the calculations of Laplace, this acceleration is confined within very restricted limits, and that a proportional diminution of speed will be certain to succeed it. So, then, the stability of the solar system would not be deranged in ages to come.

There remains but the third class, the superstitious. These worthies were not content merely to rest in ignorance; they must know all about things which had no existence whatever, and as to the moon, they had long known all about her. One set regarded her disc as a polished mirror, by means of which people could see each other and interchange their thoughts from different points of the earth. Others claimed that out of one thousand new moons that had been observed, nine hundred and fifty had been attended with remarkable disturbances, such as cataclysms, revolutions, earthquakes, the Flood itself. Then they believed in some mysterious influence exercised by her over human destinies—that every Selenite was attached to some inhabitant of the earth by a tie of sympathy; they maintained that the entire vital system is subject to her control and so on and so forth. But in time the majority renounced these vulgar errors, and espoused the true side of the question. As for the Yankees, they had no other ambition than to take possession of this new continent of the sky, and to plant upon the summit of its highest elevation the star-spangled banner of the United States.

## CHAPTER 6

# THE SAGA OF THE CANNON-BALL

The Observatory of Cambridge in its memorable letter had treated the question from a purely astronomical point of view. The mechanical part still remained.

President Barbicane had, without loss of time, nominated a Working Committee of the Gun Club. The duty of this Committee was to settle the three questions of the cannon, the projectile, and the powder. It was composed of four members of great technical knowledge, Barbicane (with a casting vote in case of equality), General Morgan, Major Elphinstone, and J. T. Maston, to whom were confided the functions of secretary. On the 8th October the Committee met at the house of President Barbicane, 3, Republican Street. The meeting was opened by the president himself.

"Gentlemen," said he, "we have to solve one of the most important problems in the whole of the noble science of gunnery. It might appear, perhaps, the most logical course to devote our first meeting to the discussion of the engine to be employed. Nevertheless, after mature consideration, it has appeared to me that the question of the projectile must take precedence of that of the cannon, and that the dimensions of the latter must necessarily depend upon those of the former."

"Suffer me to say a word," here broke in J. T. Maston. Permission having been granted, "Gentlemen," said he, with an air of inspiration, "our president is right in placing the question of the projectile above all others. The ball we are about to discharge at the moon is our ambassador to her, and I wish to consider it from a moral point of view. The cannon-ball, gentlemen, to my mind, is the most magnificent manifestation of human power. If Providence has created the stars and the planets, man has called into existence the cannon-ball. Let Providence claim the swiftness of electricity and of light, of the stars, the comets, and the planets, of wind and sound—we claim to have invented the swiftness of the cannon-ball, a hundred times superior to that of the swiftest horses or railway train. How glorious will be the moment when, infinitely exceeding all hitherto attained velocities, we shall launch our new projectile with the speed of seven miles a second! Shall it not, gentlemen—shall it not be received up there with the honours due to a terrestrial ambassador?"

Overcome with emotion the orator sat down and applied himself to a huge plate of sandwiches.

"And now," said Barbicane, "let us quit the domain of poetry and come direct to the question."

"By all means," replied the members, each with his mouth full of sandwich.

"The problem before us," continued the president, "is how to give a projectile a velocity of 12,000 yards per second. Let us at present examine the velocities hitherto attained. General Morgan will be able to enlighten us on this point."

"And the more easily," replied the general, "that during the war I was a member of the Committee of Experiments. I may say, then, that the 100-pounder Dahlgrens, which carried a distance of 5,000 yards, gave their projectile an initial velocity of 500 yards a second. The Rodman Columbiad threw a shot weighing half a ton a distance of six miles, with a velocity of 800 yards per second—a result which Armstrong and Palisser have never obtained in England."

"This," replied Barbicane, "is, I believe, the maximum velocity ever attained?"

"It is so," replied the general.

"Ah!" groaned J. T. Maston, "if my mortar had not burst——"

"Yes," quietly replied Barbicane, "but it did burst. We must take, then, for our starting-point this velocity of 800 yards. We must increase it twenty-fold. Now, reserving for later discussion the means of producing this velocity, I will call your attention to the dimensions which it will be proper to assign to the shot. You understand that we have nothing to do here with projectiles weighing at most only half a ton."

"Why not?" demanded the major.

"Because the shot," quickly replied J. T. Maston, "must be big enough to attract the attention of the inhabitants of the moon, if there are any?"

"Yes," replied Barbicane, "and for another reason more important still."

"What do you mean?" asked the major.

"I mean that it is not enough to discharge a projectile, and then take no further notice of it; we must follow it throughout its course, up to the moment when it shall reach its target."

"What?" shouted the general and the major in great surprise.

"Undoubtedly," replied Barbicane, composedly, "or our experiment would produce no result."

"But then," replied the major, "you will have to give this projectile enormous dimensions."

"No! Be so good as to listen. You know that optical instruments have acquired great perfection; with certain telescopes we have succeeded in obtaining enlargements of 6,000 times and bringing the moon within forty miles. Now, at this distance, any objects sixty feet square would be perfectly visible—but nothing smaller. If the magnifying power of telescopes has not been further increased, it is because this would lessen the brightness of the image, and the moon does not give enough light for us to see smaller objects on its surface."

"Well, then, what do you propose to do?" asked the general. "To give your projectile a diameter of sixty feet?"

"Not so."

"Do you intend, then, to increase the brightness of the moon?"

"Exactly so. If I can succeed in diminishing the density of the atmosphere through which the moon's light has to travel I shall have rendered her light more intense. To effect that, it will be enough to place a telescope on some lofty mountain. That is what we must do."

"I give up," answered the major. "You have such a way of simplifying things. And what enlargement do you expect to obtain in this way?"

"One of 48,000 times, which should bring the moon within

an apparent distance of five miles; and, in order to be visible, objects need not have a diameter of more than nine feet."

"So, then," cried J. T. Maston, "our projectile need not be more than nine feet in diameter."

"Let me observe, however," interrupted Major Elphinstone, "this will involve a weight such as——"

"My dear major," replied Barbicane, "before discussing its weight, permit me to enumerate some of the marvels which our ancestors have achieved in this respect. I don't mean to pretend that the science of gunnery has not advanced, but it is as well to bear in mind that during the middle ages they obtained results more surprising, I will venture to say, than ours. For instance, during the siege of Constantinople by Mahomet II, in 1453, stone shot of 1,900 lb. weight were employed. At Malta, in the time of the knights, there was a gun of the fortress of St. Elmo which threw a projectile weighing 2,500 lb.

"And, now, what have we seen ourselves? Armstrong guns firing shot of 500 lb., and the Rodman guns projectiles of half a ton! It seems, then, that if projectiles have gained in range, they have lost far more in weight. Now, if we turn our efforts in that direction, we ought to arrive, with the progress of science, at ten times the weight of the shot of Mahomet II, and the knights of Malta."

"Clearly," replied the major; "but what metal do you calculate upon employing?"

"Simply cast iron," said General Morgan.

"But," interrupted the Major, "since the weight of a shot is proportionate to its volume, an iron ball of nine feet in diameter would be of tremendous weight."

"Yes, if it were solid, not if it were hollow."

"Hollow? then it would be a shell?"

"Yes, a shell," replied Barbicane; "decidedly it must be. A solid shot of 108 inches would weigh more than 200,000 lb., a weight evidently far too great. Still, as we must give our projectile stability I propose to give it a weight of 20,000 lb."

"What, then, will be the thickness of the sides?" asked the major.

"If we follow the usual proportion," replied Morgan, "a diameter of 108 inches would require sides of two feet thickness, or less."

"That would be too much," replied Barbicane; "for you will bear in mind that the question is not that of a shot intended to pierce an iron plate; it will suffice, therefore, to give it sides strong enough to resist the pressure of the gas. The problem, therefore, is this— What thickness ought a cast-iron shell to have to weigh not more than 20,000 lb? Our clever secretary will soon enlighten us upon this point."

"Nothing easier," replied the worthy secretary of the Committee; and, rapidly tracing a few algebraical formulæ upon paper, among which $n^2$ and $x^2$ frequently appeared, he presently said,

"The sides will require a thickness of less than two inches."

"Will that be enough?" asked the major doubtfully.

"Clearly not!" replied the president.

"What is to be done, then?" said Elphinstone, with a puzzled air.

"Use another metal instead of iron."

"Copper?" said Morgan.

"No; that would be too heavy. I have something better than that to suggest."

"What then?" asked the major.

"Aluminium!" replied Barbicane.

"Aluminium?" cried his three colleagues in chorus.

"Unquestionably, my friends. This valuable metal possesses the whiteness of silver, the indestructibility of gold, the tenacity of iron, the fusibility of copper, the lightness of glass. It is easily wrought, is very widely distributed, forming the basis of most rocks, is three times lighter than iron, and seems to have been created for the express purpose of giving us the material for our projectile."

"But, my dear president," said the major, "is not the cost price of aluminium extremely high?"

"It was so at first discovery, but it has fallen now to nine dollars the pound."

"But still, nine dollars the pound!" replied the major, who was not willing readily to give in; "even that is an enormous price."

"Undoubtedly, my dear major; but not beyond our reach."

"What will the projectile weigh then?" asked Morgan.

"Here is the result of my calculations," replied Barbicane. "A shot of 108 inches in diameter, and 12 inches in thickness, would weigh, in cast-iron 67,440 lb.; cast in aluminium, its weight will be reduced to 19,250 lb."

"Capital!" cried the major; "but do you know that, at nine dollars the pound, this projectile would cost——"

"One hundred and seventy-three thousand and fifty dollars ($173,050). I know it quite well. But fear not, my friends; the money will not be wanting for our enterprise, I will answer for it. Now what say you to aluminium, gentlemen?"

"Adopted!" replied the three members of the Committee.

So ended the first meeting. The question of the projectile was definitely settled.

## CHAPTER 7

# HISTORY OF THE CANNON

The resolutions passed at the last meeting produced a great effect outside. Timid people took fright at the idea of a shot weighing 20,000 lb. being launched into space; they asked what cannon could ever give so high a velocity to such a mighty mass. The minutes of the second meeting were to answer such questions triumphantly. The following evening the discussion was renewed.

"My dear colleagues," said Barbicane, without further preamble, "the subject now before us is the construction of the gun, its length, its composition, and its weight. We may end by giving it gigantic dimensions; but however great may be the difficulties, our mechanical genius will readily surmount them. Be good enough, then, to give me your attention, and do not hesitate to make objections. I have no fear of them.

"The problem before us is how to give an initial force of 12,000 yards per second to a shell of 108 inches diameter, weighing 20,000 lb. Now when a projectile is launched into space, what happens to it? It is acted upon by three independent forces, the resistance of the air, the attraction of the earth, and the impetus of its discharge. Let us examine these three forces. The resistance of the air is of little importance. The atmosphere does not exceed forty miles. Now, with the given speed, the projectile will have traversed this in five seconds, and the period is too brief for the resistance of the medium to be regarded otherwise than as insignificant.

"Proceeding, then, to the attraction of the earth, the weight of the shell, we know that this weight will diminish in the inverse ratio of the square of the distance. When a body left to itself falls to the surface of the earth, it falls five feet in the first second; and if the same body were removed 257,542 miles farther off, to the distance of the moon, its fall would be reduced to about half a line in the first second.

41

That is almost equivalent to a state of perfect rest. Our business, then, is to overcome this action of gravitation. This can be accomplished by giving it a high enough initial velocity."

"There's the difficulty," broke in the major.

"True," replied the president; "but we will overcome that, for the velocity will depend upon the length of the gun and on the powder, the latter being limited only by the resisting power of the former. Our business, then, today is with the dimensions of the cannon.

"Now, up to the present time, our longest guns have not exceeded twenty-five feet in length. We shall therefore astonish the world by the dimensions we shall have to adopt. It must evidently be, then, a gun of great length, since this will increase the detention of the gas accumulated behind the projectile; but there is no advantage in passing certain limits."

"Quite so," said the major. "What is the rule in such a case?"

"Ordinarily the length of a gun is 20 to 25 times the diameter, and its weight 235 to 240 times, that of the shot."

"That is not enough," cried J. T. Maston impetuously.

"I agree with you, my good friend; and, in fact, following this proportion for a projectile nine feet in diameter, weighing 30,000 lb., the gun would only have a length of 225 feet, and a weight of 7,200,000 lb."

"Ridiculous!" rejoined Maston. "As well take a pistol."

"I think so too," replied Barbicane; "that is why I propose to quadruple that length, and to construct a gun of 900 feet."

The general and the major offered some objections; nevertheless, the proposition, strongly supported by the secretary, was definitely adopted.

"But," said Elphinstone, "what thickness must we give it?"

"A thickness of six feet," replied Barbicane.

"You surely don't think of mounting a mass like that upon a carriage?" asked the major.

"It would be a superb idea, though," said Maston.

"But impracticable, " replied Barbicane. "No; I think of sinking this engine in the earth alone, binding it with hoops of wrought iron, and finally surrounding it with a thick mass of masonry of stone and cement. The piece once cast, it must be bored with great precision, so as to preclude any possible windage. So there will be no loss whatever of gas, and all the expansive force of the powder will be used!"

"One simple question," said Elphinstone; "is our gun to be rifled?"

"No, certainly not," replied Barbicane; "we require an enormous initial velocity; and you are well aware that a shot leaves a rifled gun less rapidly than it does a smooth-bore."

"True," rejoined the major.

The Committee here adjourned for a few minutes to tea and sandwiches.

On the discussion being renewed, "Gentlemen," said Barbicane, "we must now take into consideration the metal to be employed. Our cannon must be possessed of great tenacity, great hardness, be infusible by heat, indissoluble, and inoxydable by the corrosive action of acids."

"There is no doubt about that," replied the major; "and as we shall have to employ an immense quantity of metal, we shall not be at a loss for choice."

"Well, then," said Morgan, "I propose the best alloy hitherto known, which consists of 100 parts of copper, 12 of tin, and 6 of brass."

"I admit," replied the president, "that this composition has yielded excellent results, but in the present case it would be too expensive, and very difficult to work. I think, then, that we ought to adopt a material excellent in its way and low in price, such as cast iron. What is your advice, major?"

"I quite agree with you," replied Elphinstone.

"In fact," continued Barbicane, "cast iron costs ten times less than bronze; it is easy to cast, it runs readily from the moulds of sand, it is easy to work, it is at once economical of money and time. In addition, it is excellent as a material, and I well remember that during the war, at the siege of Atlanta, some iron guns fired one thousand rounds at intervals of twenty minutes without injury."

"Cast iron is very brittle, though," replied Morgan.

"Yes, but it possesses great resistance. I will now ask our worthy secretary to calculate the weight of a cast-iron gun with a bore of nine feet and a thickness of six feet of metal."

"In a moment," replied Maston. Then, dashing off some algebraical formulæ with marvellous facility, in a minute or two he announced the following result:

"The cannon will weigh 68,040 tons. And, at two cents a pound, it will cost——"

"2,510,701 dollars."

Maston, the major, and the general regarded Barbicane uneasily.

"Well, gentlemen," replied the president, "I repeat what I said yesterday. Make yourselves easy; the millions will not be wanting."

With this assurance of their president the Committee separated, after having fixed their third meeting for the following evening.

## CHAPTER 8

# THE QUESTION OF EXPLOSIVES

There remained for consideration merely the question of the explosive. The public awaited its final decision with interest. The size of the projectile, the length of the cannon being settled, how much gunpowder would be needed?

It is generally asserted that gunpowder was invented in the fourteenth century by the monk Schwartz, who paid for his grand discovery with his life. It is, however, pretty well proved that this story ought to be ranked amongst the legends of the middle ages. Gunpowder was not invented by anyone; it was the lineal successor of the Greek fire, which, like itself, was composed of sulphur and saltpetre. Few persons are acquainted with its force. Now this is precisely what must be understood to comprehend the importance of the question submitted to the committee.

A litre of gunpowder weighs about 2 lb; during combustion it produces 400 litres of gas. This gas, on being liberated and acted upon by a temperature raised to 2,400 degrees, occupies a space of 4,000 litres; consequently the volume of powder is to the volume of gas produced by its combustion as 1 to 4,000. One may judge, therefore, of the tremendous pressure of this gas when compressed within a space of 4,000 times too small. All this was, of course, well known to the members of the committee when they met on the following evening.

The first speaker on this occasion was Major Elphinstone, who had been the director of the gunpowder factories during the war.

"Gentlemen," said this distinguished chemist, "I begin with some figures which will serve as the basis of our calculation. The old 24-pounder shot required 16 lb. of powder."

"You are certain of the amount?" broke in Barbicane.

"Quite certain," replied the major. "The Armstrong cannon needs only 75 lb. of powder for a projectile of 800 lb.,

45

and the Rodman Columbiad uses only 160 lb. of powder to send its half-ton shot a distance of six miles. These facts cannot be called in question, for I myself raised the point during the depositions taken before the Committee of Artillery."

"Quite true," said the general.

"Well," replied the major, "these figures go to prove that the quantity of powder is not increased in proportion to the weight of the shot; if a 24-pounder shot requires 16 lb. of powder—in other words, if in ordinary guns we employ a quantity of powder equal to two-thirds of the weight of the projectile, this proportion is not constant. Calculate, and you will see that in place of 333 lb. of powder, the quantity is reduced to no more than 160 lb."

"What are you aiming at?" asked the president.

"If you push your theory to extremes, my dear major," said J. T. Maston, "you will get to this, that as soon as your shot becomes sufficiently heavy you will not require any powder at all."

"Our friend Maston is always at his jokes, even in serious matters," cried the major; "but let him make his mind easy, I am going presently to propose gunpowder enough to satisfy his artillerist's propensities. I only keep to statistical facts when I say that during the war, and for the very largest guns, the weight of powder was reduced, as the result of experience, to a tenth part of the weight of the shot."

"Perfectly correct," said Morgan; "but before deciding the quantity of powder necessary, I think it would be as well——"

"We shall have to employ a large-grained powder," continued the major, "its combustion is more rapid than that of the small."

"No doubt about that," replied Morgan, "but it is very destructive, and ends by enlarging the bore of the pieces."

"Granted; but that which is injurious to a gun meant for long service is not so to our Columbiad. We shall run no danger of the gun's bursting; and our powder has to take fire instantaneously so that its mechanical effect may be complete."

"We must have," said Maston, "several touch-holes, so as to fire it at different points at the same time."

"Certainly," replied Elphinstone; "but that will render the working of the piece more difficult. I return then to my large-grained powder, which removes those difficulties. In his Columbiad charges Rodman employed a powder as large as chestnuts, made of willow charcoal, simply dried in cast-iron pans. This powder was hard and glittering, left no stain upon the hand, contained hydrogen and oxygen in large proportion, took fire instantaneously, and, though very destructive, did not noticeably injure the bore."

Up to this point Barbicane had kept aloof from the discussion; he left the others to speak while he himself listened; he had evidently got an idea. He simply said, "Well, my friends, how much powder do you propose?"

The three members looked at one another.

"Two hundred thousand pounds," said Morgan at last.

"Five hundred thousand," added the major.

"Eight hundred thousand," screamed Maston.

A moment of silence followed this triple proposal; it was at last broken by the president.

"Gentlemen," he quietly said, "I trust from this principle, that the resistance of a gun, constructed under the given conditions, is unlimited. I shall surprise our friend Maston, then, by stigmatizing his calculations as timid; and I propose to double his 800,000 lb. of powder."

"Sixteen hundred thousand pounds?" shouted Maston, leaping from his seat.

"Just so."

"We shall have to come then to my idea of a cannon half a mile long; for you see 1,600,000 lb. will occupy a space of about 20,000 cubic feet; and since the contents of your cannon do not exceed 54,000 cubic feet, it would be half full; and the bore will not be more than long enough for the gas to give enough speed to the projectile for it to reach the moon."

"Nevertheless," said the president, "I keep to that quantity. Now, 1,600,000 lb. of powder will create 6,000,000,-000 of litres of gas. Six thousand millions! You quite understand?"

"What is to be done then?" said the general.

"The thing is very simple; we must reduce this enormous quantity, while preserving its mechanical power."

"Good; but how?"

"I am going to tell you," replied Barbicane quietly. "Nothing is easier than to reduce this mass to one quarter of its bulk. You know that cellular matter which constitutes the vegetable tissue? This substance is found quite pure in many bodies, especially in cotton, which is nothing more than the down of the seeds of the cotton plant. Now, cotton, combined with cold nitric acid, becomes transformed into a substance insoluble, combustible, and highly explosive. This substance, now called pyroxyle, or fulminating cotton or gun-cotton, is prepared quite easily by simply plunging cotton for fifteen minutes into nitric acid, then washing it in water, then drying it, and it is ready for use."

"Nothing could be more simple," said Morgan.

"Moreover, pyroxyle is unaltered by moisture—a valuable property to us, inasmuch as it would take several days to load the cannon. It ignites at 170 degrees in place of 240, and its combustion is so rapid that one may set light to it on top of ordinary powder, without the latter having time to ignite."

"Perfect!" exclaimed the major.

"Only it is more expensive."

"What matter?" cried J. T. Maston.

"Finally, it gives projectiles a velocity four times greater than that of gunpowder."

"So, then, in place of 1,600,000 lb. of powder, we shall have 400,000 lb. of fulminating cotton; and as we can, without danger, compress 500 lb. of cotton into 27 cubic feet, the whole quantity will not occupy a height of more than 180 feet within the bore of the Columbiad. In this way the shot will have more than 700 feet of bore to traverse under a force of 6,000,000,000 litres of gas before taking its flight towards the moon."

At this junction J. T. Maston could not repress his emotions; he flung himself into the arms of his friend with the violence of a projectile, and Barbicane would have been stove in if he had not been bomb-proof.

This incident terminated the third meeting of the Committee.

Barbicane and his bold colleagues, to whom nothing

seemed impossible, had succeeded in solving the complex problems of projectiles, cannon, and powder. Their plan was drawn up, and it only remained to put it in execution.

"A mere matter of detail, a bagatelle," said J. T. Maston.

## CHAPTER 9

# ONE ENEMY v. 25,000,000 Friends

The American public took a lively interest in the smallest details of the enterprise of the Gun Club. It followed day by day the discussions of the committee. The most simple preparation for the great experiment, the figures which it involved, the mechanical difficulties to be solved—in two words, the whole project—roused the popular excitement to the highest pitch.

The purely scientific interest was suddenly intensified by the following incident:

We have seen what legions of admirers and friends Barbicane's project had rallied round its author. There was, however, one individual who, alone in all the States of the Union, protested against the project of the Gun Club. He attacked it furiously on every opportunity, and human nature is such that Barbicane felt more keenly the opposition of that one man than he did the applause of all the others. He was well aware of the motive of this antipathy, the origin of this solitary enmity, the cause of this long-standing personal animosity and the rivalry in which it had its rise.

The President of the Gun Club had never seen this persevering enemy. Fortunate that it was so, for a meeting between the two men would certainly have been attended with serious consequences. This rival was a man of science, like Barbicane himself, of a fiery, daring and violent disposition; a pure Yankee. His name was Captain Nicholl; he lived at Philadelphia.

Most people are aware of the curious struggle which arose during the Federal war between the guns and the armour of iron-plated ships. The result was the entire reconstruction of the navies of both the antagonists; as the one grew heavier, the other became thicker in proportion. The *Merrimac*, the *Monitor*, the *Tennessee*, the *Wackhausen* discharged enormous projectiles themselves, after having

50

been armour-clad against the projectiles of others. In fact they did to others that which they would *not* they should do to them—that grand principle of immorality upon which rests the whole art of war.

Now if Barbicane was a great founder of shot, Nicholl was a great forger of plates; the one cast night and day at Baltimore, the other forged day and night at Philadelphia. As soon as ever Barbicane invented a new shot, Nicholl invented a new plate, each followed a sequence of ideas essentially opposed to the other. Happily for these citizens, so useful to their country, a distance of from fifty to sixty miles separated them, and they had never met. Which of these two inventors had the advantage over the other was difficult to decide. By all accounts, however, it would seem that the armour-plate would in the end have to give way to the shot; nevertheless, there were competent judges who had their doubts on the point.

At the last experiment the cylindro-conical projectiles of Barbicane stuck like so many pins in the Nicholl plates. On that day the Philadelphian iron-forger believed himself victorious, and could not evince enough contempt for his rival; but when the other afterwards substituted for conical shot simple 600 lb. shells, at very moderate velocity, the captain was obliged to give in: these projectiles knocked his best metal plate to shivers.

Matters were at this stage, and victory seemed to rest with the shot, when the war came to an end on the very day when Nicholl had completed a new armour-plate of wrought steel. It was a masterpiece of its kind, and bid defiance to all the projectiles in the world. The captain had it conveyed to the Polygon at Washington, challenging the President of the Gun Club to smash it. Barbicane, peace having been declared, declined to try the experiment.

Nicholl, now furious, offered to expose his plate to the shock of any shot, solid, hollow, round, or conical. Refused by the president, who did not choose to compromise his last success.

Nicholl, disgusted by this obstinacy, tried to tempt Barbicane by offering him every chance. He proposed to fix the plate with two hundred yards of the gun. Barbicane still obstinate in refusal. A hundred yards? Not even *seventy-five!*

"At fifty then!" roared the captain through the newspapers. "At twenty-five yards ! ! and I'll stand behind it ! ! !"

Barbicane returned for answer that, even if Captain Nicholl would be so good as to stand in front, he would not fire any more.

Nicholl could not contain himself at this reply; he threw out hints of cowardice; that a man who refused to fire a cannon-shot was pretty near being afraid of it; that artillerists who fight at six miles' distance are substituting mathematical formulæ for individual courage.

To these insinuations Barbicane returned no answer; perhaps he never heard of them, so absorbed was he in the calculations for his great enterprise.

When the famous communication was made to the Gun Club, the captain's wrath passed all bounds; with his intense jealousy was mingled a feeling of absolute impotence. How was he to invent anything to beat this 900-feet Columbiad? What armour-plate could ever resist a projectile of 30,000 lb. weight? Overwhelmed at first under this violent shock, he by and by recovered himself, and resolved to crush the proposal by the weight of his arguments.

He then violently attacked the labours of the Gun Club, published a number of letters in the newspapers, endeavoured to prove Barbicane ignorant of the first principles of gunnery. He maintained that it was absolutely impossible to give anything whatever a velocity of 12,000 yards per second; that even with such a velocity a projectile of such a weight could not transcend the limits of the earth's atmosphere. Further still, even regarding the velocity to be acquired, and granting it to be sufficient, the shell could not resist the pressure of the gas developed by the ignition of 1,600,000 lb. of powder; and supposing it to resist that pressure, it would be the less able to support that temperature; it would melt on quitting the Columbiad, and fall back in a red-hot shower upon the heads of the imprudent spectators.

Barbicane continued his work without regarding these attacks.

Nicholl then took up the question in its other aspects.

Without touching upon its uselessness in all points of view, he regarded the experiment as fraught with extreme danger, both to the citizens who might sanction by their presence so reprehensible a spectacle, and also to the towns in the neighbourhood of this deplorable cannon. He also observed that if the projectile did not succeed in reaching its destination (a result absolutely impossible), it must inevitably fall back upon the earth, and that the shock of such a mass, multiplied by the square of its velocity, would seriously endanger every point of the globe. In the circumstances, therefore, and without interfering with the rights of free citizens, it was a case for the intervention of Government, which ought not to endanger the safety of all for the pleasure of one individual.

Spite of all his arguments, however, Captain Nicholl remained alone in his opinion. Nobody listened to him, and he did not succeed in alienating a single admirer from the President of the Gun Club. The latter did not even take the pains to refute the arguments of his rival.

Nicholl, driven into his last entrenchments, and not able to fight personally in the cause, resolved to fight with money. He published, therefore, in the *Richmond Inquirer* a series of wagers, conceived in these terms, and on an increasing scale:

No. 1. (1,000 dols.)—That the necessary funds for the experiment of the Gun Club will not be forthcoming.

No. 2. (2,000 dols.)—That the operation of casting a cannon of 900 feet is impracticable, and cannot possibly succeed.

No. 3. (3,000 dols.)—That it is impossible to load the Columbiad, and that the pyroxyle will take fire spontaneously under the pressure of the projectile.

No. 4. (4,000 dols.)—That the Columbiad will burst at the first fire.

No. 5. (5,000 dols.)—That the shot will not travel farther than six miles, and that it will fall back again a few seconds after its discharge.

It was an important sum, therefore, which the captain risked in his invincible obstinacy. He had no less than 15,000 dollars at stake.

Notwithstanding the importance of the challenge, on the 19th May he received a sealed packet containing the following superbly laconic reply:

"BALTIMORE, OCT. 19

"Done.

"BARBICANE."

# FLORIDA AND TEXAS

One question yet remained to be decided: to choose a favourable spot for the experiment. According to the advice of the Observatory of Cambridge, the gun must be fired perpendicularly to the plane of the horizon, towards the zenith. Now the moon does not traverse the zenith, except in places situated between 0° and 28° of latitude. It became, then, necessary to decide exactly that spot on the globe where the immense Columbiad should be cast.

On the 20th October, at a general meeting of the Gun Club, Barbicane produced a magnificent map of the United States. "Gentlemen," said he, in opening the discussion, "I presume that we are all agreed that this experiment cannot and ought not to be tried anywhere but within the Union. Now, by good fortune, certain frontiers of the United States extend downwards as far as the 28th parallel of the north latitude. If you will cast your eye over this map, you will see that we have at our disposal the whole of the southern portion of Texas and Florida."

It was finally agreed, then, that the Columbiad must be cast in either Texas or Florida. The result, however, of this decision was to create a rivalry entirely without precedent between the different towns of these two states.

The 28th parallel, on reaching the American coast, traverses the peninsula of Florida, dividing it into two nearly equal portions. Then, plunging into the Gulf of Mexico, it subtends the arc formed by the coast of Alabama, Mississippi, and Louisiana, then skirting Texas, off which it cuts a corner, it continues its course over Mexico, crosses the Sonora, Old California, and loses itself in the Pacific Ocean. It was, therefore, only those portions of Texas and Florida which were situated below this parallel which came within the prescribed conditions of latitude.

Florida, in its southern part, claims no cities of importance; it is studded only with forts raised against the roving Indians. One solitary town, Tampa Town, was able to put in a claim in favour of its situation.

In Texas, on the contrary, the towns are much more numerous and important; they formed an imposing league against the claims of Florida. So scarcely was the decision known when the Texan and Floridan deputies arrived at Baltimore in an incredibly short space of time. From that very moment President Barbicane and the influential members of the Gun Club were beseiged day and night by formidable claims. If seven cities of Greece contended for the honour of having given birth to Homer, here were two entire states threatening to come to blows about the cannon.

The rival parties promenaded the streets with arms in their hands; and at every occasion of their meeting a clash was to be apprehended which might have been attended with disastrous results. Happily the prudence and address of President Barbicane averted the danger. These personal demonstrations found sponsors in the newspapers of the different states. The *New York Herald* and the *Tribune* supported Texas, while the *Times* and the *American Review* espoused the cause of the Floridan Deputies. The members of the Gun Club could not decide to which to give the preference.

Texas produced its array of twenty-six counties; Florida replied that twelve counties were better than twenty-six in a country only one-sixth as large.

Texas plumed itself upon its 330,000 natives; Florida, with a far smaller territory, boasted of being much more densely populated with 56,000.

The Texans, through the columns of the *Herald*, claimed that some regard should be had to a state which grew the best cotton in all America, produced the best green oak for the service of the navy, and contained the finest oil, as well as iron mines, in which the yield was 50 per cent. of pure metal.

To this the *American Review* replied that the soil of Florida, although not equally rich, afforded the best conditions for the moulding and casting of the Columbiad, consisting as it did of sand and argillaceous earth.

"That may be all very well," replied the Texans; "but you must first get to this country. Now the communications with Florida are difficult, while the coast of Texas offers the bay of Galveston, which possesses a circumference of fourteen leagues, and is capable of containing the navies of the entire world!"

"A pretty notion truly," replied the papers in the interest of Florida, "that of Galveston Bay, *below the 29th parallel!* Have *we* not got the bay of Espiritu Santo, opening precisely upon the *28th degree,* and by which ships can reach Tampa Town direct?"

"A fine bay! half choked with sand!" "Choked yourselves!" returned the others.

Thus the war went on for several days, when Florida endeavoured to draw her adversary on to fresh ground; and one morning the *Times* hinted that, the enterprise being essentially American, it ought not to be attempted upon other than purely American territory.

To these words Texas retorted, "American! are we not as much Americans as you? Were not Texas and Florida both incorporated into the Union in 1845?"

"Undoubtedly," replied the *Times*; "but we have belonged to the Americans ever since 1820."

"Yes!" returned the *Tribune*; "after having been Spaniards or English for 200 years, you were sold to the United States for five million dollars!"

"Well! and why need we blush for that? Was not Louisiana bought from Napoleon in 1803 at the price of sixteen million dollars?"

"Scandalous!" roared the Texan deputies. "A wretched little strip of country like Florida to dare to compare itself to Texas, who, in place of selling herself, asserted her own independence, drove out the Mexicans in March 2, 1836, and declared herself a federal republic after the victory gained by Samuel Houston, on the banks of the San Jacinto, over the troops of Santa Anna!—a country, in fine, which voluntarily annexed itself to the United States of America!"

"Yes; because it was afraid of the Mexicans!" replied Florida.

"Afraid!" From this moment the state of things became

intolerable. A sanguinary encounter seemed daily imminent between the two parties in the streets of Baltimore. It became necessary to keep an eye upon the deputies.

President Barbicane knew not which way to look. Notes, documents, letters full of menaces showered down upon his house. Which side ought he to take? As regarded the suitability of the soil, the facility of communication, the rapidity of transport, the claims of both states were evenly balanced. As for political prepossessions, they had nothing to do with the question.

This deadlock had existed for some little time when Barbicane resolved to get rid of it at once. He called a meeting of his colleagues, and laid before them a proposition which, it will be seen, was profoundly sagacious.

"On carefully considering," he said, "what is going on now between Florida and Texas, it is clear that the same difficulties will recur with all the towns of the favoured state. The rivalry will descend from state to city, and so on downwards. Now Texas possesses *eleven* towns within the prescribed conditions, which will further dispute the honour and create us new enemies, while Florida has only *one*. I go in, therefore, for Florida and Tampa Town."

This decision, on being made known, utterly crushed the Texan deputies. Seized with an indescribable fury, they addressed threatening letters to the different members of the Gun Club by name. The magistrates had but one course to take, and they took it. They chartered a special train, forced the Texans into it whether they would or no; and they quitted the city with a speed of thirty miles an hour.

Quickly, however, as they were despatched, they found time to hurl one last and bitter sarcasm at their adversaries.

Alluding to the extent of Florida, a mere peninsula confined between two seas, they declared that it could never sustain the shock of the discharge, and that it would "bust up" at the very first shot.

The Floridans replied with a brevity worthy of ancient Sparta: "Very well, let it bust!"

## CHAPTER 11

# URBI ET ORBI

The astronomical, mechanical, and topographical difficulties resolved, finally came the question of finance. The sum required was far too great for any individual, or even any single state, to provide.

President Barbicane undertook, despite the matter's being a purely American affair, to render it one of universal interest, and to request the financial co-operation of all peoples. It was, he maintained, the right and the duty of the whole earth to interfere in the affairs of its satellite. The subscription opened at Baltimore extended to the whole world—*Urbi et orbi*.

This subscription was successful beyond all expectation; notwithstanding that it was a question not of *lending* but of *giving* the money. It was a purely disinterested operation in the strictest sense of the term, and offered not the slightest chance of profit.

The effect, however, of Barbicane's communication was not confined to the frontiers of the United States; it crossed the Atlantic and Pacific, invading simultaneously Asia and Europe, Africa and Oceania. The observatories of the Union placed themselves in immediate communication with those of foreign countries. Some transmitted their good wishes; the rest maintained a prudent silence, quietly awaiting the result. As for the observatory at Greenwich, seconded as it was by the twenty-two astronomical establishments of Great Britain, it spoke plainly enough. It boldly denied the possibility of success, and pronounced in favour of the theories of Captain Nicholl. But this was nothing more than mere English jealousy.

On the 8th October President Barbicane published a manifesto full of enthusiasm, in which he made an appeal to "all persons of good will upon the face of the earth." This document, translated into all languages, met with immense success.

Subscription lists were opened in all the principal cities of the Union, with a central office at the Baltimore Bank, 9, Baltimore Street.

In addition, subscriptions were received at the principal banks in the two continents.

Three days after the manifesto of President Barbicane, 4,000,000 of dollars were paid into the towns of the Union. With such a balance the Gun Club might begin operations at once. But some days later advices were received to the effect that the foreign subscriptions were being eagerly taken up. Certain countries distinguished themselves by their liberality; others untied their purse-strings with less facility —a matter of temperament.

There remained but England; and we know the contemptuous antipathy with which she received Barbicane's proposition. The English have but one soul for all the inhabitants which Great Britain contains. They hinted that the enterprise of the Gun Club was contrary to the "principle of nonintervention." And they did not subscribe a single farthing.

At this intimation the Gun Club merely shrugged its shoulders and returned to its great work. When the countries of South America had poured forth their quota into its hands, the sum of 300,000 dollars, it found itself in possession of a considerable capital, of which the following is a statement:—

| | | |
|---|---|---|
| United States subscriptions . . . | 4,000,000 | dollars |
| Foreign subscriptions . . . . . | 1,446,675 | " |
| Total . . . . | 5,446,675 | " |

Such was the sum which the public poured into the treasury of the Gun Club.

Let no one be surprised at the size of the amount. The work of casting, boring, masonry, the transport of workmen, their establishment in an almost uninhabited country, the construction of furnaces and workshops, the plant, the powder, the projectile, and incidental expenses, would, according to the estimates, absorb nearly the whole. Certain cannon shots in the Federal war cost 1,000 dollars apiece. This one of President Barbicane, unique in the annals of gunnery, might well cost five thousand times more.

On the 20th October a contract was entered into with the manufactory of Goldspring, near New York, which during the war had furnished Parratt with the best cast-iron guns. It was stipulated between the contracting parties that the manufactory of Goldspring should engage to transport to Tampa Town, in southern Florida, the necessary materials for casting the Columbiad. The work was bound to be completed at latest by the 15th October following, and the cannon delivered in good condition under penalty of a forfeit of 100 dollars a day to the moment when the moon should again present herself under the same conditions—in eighteen years and eleven days.

The engagement of the workmen, their pay, and all the necessary details of the work, devolved upon the Goldspring Company.

This contract, executed in duplicate, was signed by Barbicane, President of the Gun Club, of the one part, and T. Murchison, director of the Goldspring manufactory, of the other.

## CHAPTER 12

# STONES HILL

When the decision was arrived at by the Gun Club, to the disparagement of Texas, everyone in America, where reading is a universal acquirement, set to work to study the geography of Florida. Never before had there been such a sale for works like *Bertram's Travels in Florida*, *Roman's Natural History of East and West Florida*, *William's Territory of Florida*, and *Cleveland on the Cultivation of the Sugar-Cane in Florida*. It became necessary to issue fresh editions of them.

Barbicane had something better to do than to read. He wanted to see things with his own eyes, and to decide the exact position of the proposed gun. So, without a moment's loss of time, he placed at the disposal of the Cambridge Observatory the funds necessary for the construction of a telescope, and entered into negotiations with the house of Breadwill and Co., of Albany, for the construction of an aluminium projectile of the necessary size. He then quitted Baltimore, accompanied by J. T. Maston, Major Elphinstone, and the manager of the Goldspring Factory.

On the following day, the four fellow-travellers arrived at New Orleans. There they immediately embarked on board the *Tampico*, a despatch-boat belonging to the Federal navy, which the Government had placed at their disposal; and, getting up steam, they watched the banks of Louisiana speedily disappear from sight.

The passage was not long. Two days after starting, the *Tampico*, having made four hundred and eighty miles, came in sight of the coast of Florida. On a nearer approach Barbicane found himself in view of a low, flat country of somewhat barren aspect. After coasting along a series of creeks abounding in lobsters and oysters, the *Tampico* entered the bay of Espiritu Santo, where she finally anchored in a small natural harbour, formed by the *embouchure* of the River Hillisborough, at seven p.m. on the 22nd October.

Our four passengers disembarked at once. "Gentlemen," said Barbicane, "we have no time to lose; to-morrow we must obtain horses, and proceed to reconnoitre the country."

Barbicane had scarcely set his foot on shore when three thousand of the inhabitants of Tampa Town came forth to meet him, an honour due to the president who had honoured their country by his choice.

Declining, however, every kind of ovation, Barbicane ensconced himself in a room of the Franklin Hotel.

On the morrow some of those small horses of the Spanish breed, full of vigour and of fire, stood snorting under his windows; but instead of *four* steeds, here were *fifty*, together with their riders. Barbicane descended with his three fellow-travellers; and much astonished were they all to find themselves in the midst of such a cavalcade. He noticed that every horseman carried a carbine slung across his shoulders and pistols in his holsters.

On expressing his surprise at these preparations, he was speedily enlightened by a young Floridan, who quietly said,

"Sir, there are Seminoles there."

"What do you mean by Seminoles?"

"Savages who scour the prairies. We thought it best, therefore, to escort you on your road."

"Pooh!" cried J. T. Maston, mounting his steed.

"All right," said the Floridan; "but it is true enough, nevertheless."

"Gentlemen," answered Barbicane, "I thank you for your kind attention; but it is time to be off."

It was five a.m. when Barbicane and his party, quitting Tampa Town, made their way along the coast in the direction of Alifia Creek, a little river which falls into Hillisborough Bay twelve miles above the Town. Barbicane and his escort coasted its right bank to the eastward. Soon the waves of the bay disappeared behind a bend of rising ground, and the Floridan countryside alone offered itself to view.

Florida, discovered on Palm Sunday, in 1512, by Juan Ponce de Leon, was originally named *Pascha Florida*. It little deserved that designation with its dry and parched coasts. But after some few miles of tract the nature of the soil gradually changes and the country shows itself worthy of the name.

Barbicane appeared highly pleased on observing the progressive rising of the ground; and in answer to a question of J. T. Maston, he replied:

"My worthy friend, we cannot do better than sink our Columbiad in these higher regions."

"To get nearer to the moon, perhaps?" said the secretary of the Gun Club.

"Not exactly," replied Barbicane, smiling; "do you not see that amongst these elevated plateaux we shall have much easier work? No struggles with the water-springs, which will save us long and expensive draining operations; and we shall be working in daylight instead of down a deep and narrow well. Our business, then, is to start excavating upon ground some hundreds of yards above sea level."

"You are right, sir," struck in Murchison, the engineer; "and, if I'm not mistaken we shall soon find a suitable site."

"I wish we were making the first stroke of the pickaxe," said the president.

"And I wish we were making the *last*," cried J. T. Maston.

About ten a.m. the little band had crossed a dozen miles. To fertile plains succeeded a region of forests. There perfumes of the most varied kinds mingled together in tropical profusion, whose blossoms and fruits rivalled each other in colour and perfume. Beneath the odorous shade of these magnificent trees fluttered and warbled a little world of brilliantly plumaged birds.

J. T. Maston and the major could not repress their admiration on finding themselves in presence of the glorious beauties of this wealth of nature. President Barbicane, however, less sensitive to these wonders, was in haste to press forward; the very luxuriance of the country displeased him. They hastened onwards, therefore, and were compelled to ford several rivers, not without danger, for they were infested with huge alligators from fifteen to eighteen feet long. Maston courageously menaced them with his steel hook, but he only succeeded in frightening some pelicans and teal, while tall flamingos stared stupidly at the party.

At length these denizens of the swamps disappeared in their turn; smaller trees became thinly scattered among less dense thickets—a few isolated groups detached in the midst of endless plains over which ranged herds of startled deer.

"At last," cried Barbicane, rising in his stirrups, "here we are at the region of pines!"

"Yes! and of savages too," replied the major.

In fact, some Seminoles had just come in sight upon the horizon, they rode violently backwards and forwards on their fleet horses, brandishing their spears or discharging their guns with a dull report. These hostile demonstrations, however, had no effect upon Barbicane and his companions.

They were then at the centre of a rocky plain, which the sun scorched with its parching rays. This was formed by a considerable rise of the soil, which seemed to offer the members of the Gun Club all the conditions needed for the construction of their Columbiad.

"Halt!" said Barbicane, reining up. "Has this place any name?"

"It is called Stones Hill," replied one of the Floridans.

Barbicane, without saying a word, dismounted, seized his instruments, and began to note his position with extreme exactness. The little band, drawn up behind him, watched his proceedings in profound silence.

At this moment the sun passed the meridian. Barbicane, after a few moments, jotted down the result of his observations, and said:

"This spot is situated 1,800 feet above the level of the sea, in 27° 7′ N. lat. and 5° 7′ W. long. of the meridian of Washington. Its rocky and barren character seems to offer all we need for our experiment. On that plain will be raised our magazines, workshops, furnaces, and workmen's huts; and here, from this very spot," he continued stamping his foot on the summit of Stones Hill, "hence our projectile shall take its flight into the regions of the Solar World."

## CHAPTER 13

# PICKAXE AND TROWEL

The same evening Barbicane and his companions returned to Tampa Town; and Murchison, the engineer, re-embarked on board the *Tampico* for New Orleans. His object was to enlist an army of workmen, and to collect together the greater part of the materials. The members of the Gun Club remained at Tampa Town, to begin the preliminary works with the aid of the people of the country.

Eight days after its departure, the *Tampico* returned into the bay of Espiritu Santo, with a whole flotilla of steam-boats. Murchison had succeeded in getting together fifteen hundred artisans. Attracted by the high pay and large boun-ties offered by the Gun Club, a choice legion of stokers, iron-founders, lime-burners, miners, brickmakers, and arti-sans of every trade, had been enlisted without distinction of colour. As many of these people brought their families with them, their departure resembled an emigration.

On the 31st October, at ten o'clock in the morning, the troop disembarked on the quays of Tampa Town; and one may imagine the activity which pervaded that little town, whose population was thus doubled in a single day.

During the first few days they were busy discharging the cargo brought by the flotilla, the machines, and the rations, as well as a large number of huts constructed of iron plates, separately pieced and numbered. At the same period Bar-bicane laid the first sleepers of a railway fifteen miles in length, to unite Stones Hill with Tampa Town. On the 1st November Barbicane quitted the town with a detachment of workmen; and on the following day the whole town of huts was erected round Stones Hill. This they enclosed with palisades; and as regards energy and activity, it might have shortly been mistaken for one of the great cities of the Union. Everything was placed under a complete system of discipline, and the works were commenced in most perfect order.

The nature of the soil having been carefully examined by repeated borings, the work of excavation was fixed for the 4th November.

On that day Barbicane called together his foremen and addressed them: "You are well aware, my friends, of the object with which I have assembled you together in this wild part of Florida. Our business is to construct a cannon measuring nine feet in its interior diameter, six feet thick, and with a stone revetment of nineteen and a half feet in thickness. We have, therefore, to dig a well sixty feet in diameter down to a depth of nine hundred feet. This great work must be completed *within eight months*, so that you have 2,543,400 cubic feet of earth to excavate in 255 days; in round numbers, 2,000 cubic feet per day. That which would present no difficulty to a thousand navvies working in open country will be of course more troublesome in a comparatively confined space. However, the thing must be done, and I reckon for its accomplishment upon your courage as much as upon your skill."

At eight o'clock in the morning the first stroke of the pickaxe was struck upon the soil in Florida; and from that moment that prince of tools was never inactive for one moment in the hands of the excavators. The gangs relieved each other every three hours.

On the 4th November fifty workmen commenced digging, in the very centre of the enclosed space on the summit of Stones Hill, a circular hole sixty feet in diameter. The pickaxe first struck upon a black earth, six inches in thickness, which was speedily disposed of. To this earth succeeded two feet of fine sand, which was carefully laid aside as being valuable for the casting of the inner mould. After the sand appeared some compact white clay, resembling chalk, which extended down to a depth of four feet. Then the iron of the picks struck upon the hard subsoil; a kind of rock formed of petrified shells, very dry, very solid, which the picks could penetrate with difficulty. At this point the excavation attained a depth of six feet and a half, and the work of the masonry was begun.

At the bottom of this excavation they constructed a wheel of oak, a circle strongly bolted together, and of immense strength. The centre of this wooden disc was hollowed out to a diameter equal to the exterior diameter of the Columbiad. Upon this wheel rested the first layers of the masonry, the stones of which were bound together with irresistible tenacity by hydraulic cement. The workmen, after laying the stones from the circumference to the centre, were thus enclosed within a well twenty-one feet in diameter. When this work was accomplished, the miners resumed their picks and cut away the rock from underneath the wheel itself, taking care to support it as they advanced upon blocks of great thickness. At every two feet which the hole gained in depth they successively withdrew the blocks. The wheel then sank little by little, and with it the massive ring of masonry, on the upper bed of which the masons laboured incessantly, always reserving some vent holes to permit the escape of gas during the operation of casting.

This kind of work required extreme nicety and minute attention on the part of the workmen. More than one, in digging underneath the wheel, was dangerously injured by the splinters of stone. But their ardour never relaxed, night or day. By day they worked under the rays of the scorching sun; by night under the gleam of the electric light. The sounds of the picks against the rock, the bursting of the mines, the grinding of the machines, the wreaths of smoke scattered through the air, traced around Stones Hill a circle of terror which the herds of buffaloes and the war parties of the Seminoles never ventured to pass. Nevertheless, the works advanced regularly, as the steam-cranes rapidly removed the soil. Unexpected obstacles were of little account; and with regard to foreseen difficulties, they were speedily disposed of.

At the end of the first month the well had attained the depth specified, 112 feet. This depth was doubled in December, and trebled in January.

During February the workmen had to contend with a sheet of water which made its way right through the outer soil. They had to use very powerful pumps and compressed-air engines to drain it off, to close up the opening just as one stops a leak on board ship. They at last succeeded in getting the upper hand of these streams; only, because of the loosening of the soil, the wheel partly gave way, caus-

ing a slight partial settlement. This accident cost the life of
several workmen.

No other occurrence arrested the progress of the operation; and on the 10th June, twenty days before the expira-
tion of the period fixed by Barbicane, the well, lined
throughout with its facing of stone, had attained the depth
of 900 feet. At the bottom the masonry rested upon a massive block measuring thirty feet in thickness, while its upper
surface was level with the surrounding soil.

President Barbicane and the members of the Gun Club
warmly congratulated their engineer Murchison: the cyclo-
pean work had been accomplished with extraordinary speed.

During these eight months Barbicane never quitted
Stones Hill for a single instant. Keeping ever close to the
excavation, he busied himself incessantly with the welfare
and health of his workpeople, and was singularly fortunate
in warding off the epidemics common to large communities
of men, and so disastrous in those regions of the globe which
are exposed to the influences of tropical climates.

Many workmen, it is true, paid with their lives for the
rashness inherent in these dangerous labours; but these mis-
haps cannot be avoided, and they are classed amongst details with which the Americans trouble themselves but little. They have in fact more regard for human nature in general than for the individual in particular.

Nevertheless, Barbicane held very different views and put
them in force at every opportunity. So, thanks to his care,
his intelligence, his useful intervention in all difficulties, his
prodigious and humane sagacity, the average of accidents
did not exceed that of the European countries noted for their
excessive precautions, France, for instance, among others,
where they reckon about one accident for every two hundred thousand francs of work.

## CHAPTER 14

# THE FETE OF THE CASTING

During the eight months employed in the excavation the preparatory works of the casting had simultaneously been carried on with extreme rapidity. A stranger arriving at Stones Hill would have been surprised at the spectacle offered to his view.

At 600 yards from the well, and circularly arranged around it rose 1,200 reverberating ovens, each six feet in diameter, and separated from each other by an interval of three feet. The circumference occupied by these 1,200 ovens was two miles. Being all constructed on the same plan, each with its high quadrangular chimney, they produced a most singular effect.

It will be remembered that on their third meeting the Committee had decided to use cast-iron for the Columbiad, and in particular the *white* description. This metal is the most tenacious, the most ductile, and the most malleable, and consequently the most suitable for all moulding operations; and when smelted with pit coal, it is of superior quality for all engineering works requiring great resisting power, such as cannon, steam-boilers, hydraulic presses, and the like.

Cast-iron, however, if subjected to only one single fusion, is rarely sufficiently homogeneous; and it requires a second fusion to refine it completely by freeing it from its last earthly impurities. So before being forwarded to Tampa Town, the iron ore, smelted in the great furnaces of Goldspring, and brought into contact with coal and silica heated to a high temperature, was carburized and transformed into cast-iron. After this first operation, the metal was sent on to Stones Hill.

They had, however, to deal with 136,000,000 lb. of iron, a quantity far too costly to send by railway: the cost would have been double that of the material. It appeared prefer-

able to freight vessels at New York, and to load them with
the iron in bars. This, however, required not less than sixty-
eight vessels of 1,000 tons, a veritable fleet, which, quitting
New York on the 3rd May, on the 10th of the same month
ascended the Bay of Espiritu Santo, and discharged the
cargoes, without dues, in the port of Tampa Town. Thence
the iron was transported by rail to Stones Hill, and about
the middle of January this enormous mass of metal was delivered at its destination.

It will be readily understood that 1,200 furnaces were
not too many to melt simultaneously these 60,000 tons of
iron. Each contained nearly 140,000 lb. weight of metal;
built after the model of those which cast the Rodman gun,
they were trapezoidal in shape, with a high elliptical arch.
These furnaces, constructed of fireproof brick, were especially adapted for burning pit coal, with a flat bottom upon
which the iron bars were laid. This bottom, inclined at an
angle of 25°, allowed the metal to flow into the receiving
troughs; and the 1,200 converging trenches carried the molten metal down to the central well.

The day following that on which the masonry and the
boring had been completed, Barbicane set to work upon the
central mould. His object was now to raise within the centre
of the well, and with a coincident axis, a cylinder 900 feet
high, and 9 feet in diameter, which should exactly fill the
space reserved for the bore of the Columbiad. This cylinder
was composed of a mixture of clay and sand, with the addition of a little hay and straw. The space left between the
mould and the masonry was to be filled by the molten metal,
which would thus form a vertical tube with walls six feet
thick. This cylinder, to maintain its equilibrium, had to be
bound by iron bands, and firmly fixed at intervals by cross-
clamps fastened into the stone lining; after the casting these
would be buried in the block of metal, leaving no external
projection.

This operation was completed on the 8th July, and the
run of metal fixed for the following day.

"This fête of the casting will be a grand ceremony," said
J. T. Maston to his friend Barbicane.

"Undoubtedly," said Barbicane; "but it will not be a
public fête."

"What! will you not open the gates of the enclosure to all comers?"

"I must be very careful, Maston. The casting of the Columbiad is an extremely delicate, not to say a dangerous, operation, and I should prefer its being done privately. At the discharge of the projectile, a fête if you like—till then, no!"

The president was right. The operation involved unforeseen dangers, which a great influx of spectators would have hindered him from averting. It was necessary to preserve complete freedom of movement. No one was admitted within the enclosure except a delegation of members of the Gun Club, who had made the voyage to Tampa Town. Among these was the brisk Bilsby, Tom Hunter, Colonel Blomsberry, Major Elphinstone, General Morgan and others to whom the casting of the Columbiad was a matter of personal interest. J. T. Maston became their cicerone. He omitted no detail; he conducted them throughout the magazines, workshops, through the midst of the engines, and made them visit the whole 1,200 furnaces one after the other. At the end of the twelve-hundredth visit they were pretty well knocked up.

The casting was to take place at 12 o'clock precisely. The previous evening each furnace had been charged with 114,000 lb. of metal in bars disposed cross-ways to each other, so as to allow the hot air to circulate freely between them. At daybreak the 1,200 chimneys vomited their torrents of flame into the air, and the ground was agitated with dull tremblings. As many pounds of metal as there were to *cast*, so many pounds of coal were there to *burn*. Thus there were 68,000 tons of coal, which projected in the face of the sun a thick curtain of smoke.

The heat soon became insupportable within the circle of furnaces, whose rumbling resembled the rolling of thunder. The powerful ventilators added their continuous blasts and saturated the glowing plates with oxygen. The operation, to be successful, had to be carried out with great rapidity. On a signal given by a cannon-shot each furnace was to give vent to the molten iron and to empty itself completely. These arrangements made, foreman and workman waited the preconcerted moment with impatience mingled with a certain emotion. Not a soul remained within the enclosure. Each superintendent took his post by the aperture of the run.

Barbicane and his colleagues, perched on a neighbouring eminence, were present at the operation. In front of them was a piece of artillery ready to fire on the signal from the engineer. Some minutes before midday the first driblets of metal began to flow; the reservoirs filled little by little; and when the whole melting was complete it was held in abeyance for a few minutes to facilitate the separation of foreign substances.

Twelve o'clock struck! A gun-shot suddenly pealed forth and shot its flame into the air. Twelve hundred melting-troughs were simultaneously opened and twelve hundred fiery serpents, unrolling their incandescent curves, crept towards the central well. They plunged down with a terrific noise to a depth of 900 feet. It was an exciting and a magnificent spectacle. The ground trembled, while these molten waves, launching into the sky their wreaths of smoke, evaporated the moisture of the mould and hurled it upwards through the vent-holes of the stone lining in dense vapour-clouds, which unrolled their thick spirals to a height of 1,000 yards into the air. A savage, wandering somewhere beyond the limits of the horizon, might have believed that some new crater was forming in the bosom of Florida, although there was neither any eruption, nor typhoon, nor storm, nor struggle of the elements, nor any of those terrible phenomena which nature can produce. No, it was man alone who had produced these reddish vapours, these gigantic flames worthy of a volcano, these tremendous vibrations resembling the shock of an earthquake, these reverberations rivalling those of hurricanes and storms; and it was his hand which precipitated into an abyss, dug by himself, a whole Niagara of molten metal!

## CHAPTER 15

# THE COLUMBIAD

Had the casting succeeded? The engineers were reduced to mere conjecture. There was indeed every reason to expect success, since the mould had absorbed the entire mass of the molten metal; still some considerable time must elapse before they could arrive at any certainty upon the matter.

During this time the patience of the members of the Gun Club was sorely tried. But they could do nothing. J. T. Maston escaped roasting by a miracle. Fifteen days after the casting an immense column of smoke was still rising in the open sky, and the ground burnt the soles of the feet within a radius of 200 feet round the summit of Stones Hill. It was impossible to approach nearer. All they could do was to wait with what patience they might.

"Here we are at the 10th August," exclaimed J. T. Maston one morning, "only four months to the 1st December! We shall never be ready in time!" Barbicane said nothing, but his silence covered serious irritation.

However, daily observations revealed a change going on in the ground. About the 15th August the vapours ejected had plainly lessened in intensity and thickness. Some days afterwards the earth exhaled only a slight puff of smoke, the last breath of the monster enclosed within its circle of stone. Little by little the belt of heat contracted, until on the 22nd August Barbicane, his colleagues, and the engineer were able to set foot on the iron surface which lay level upon the summit of Stones Hill.

"At last!" exclaimed the President of the Gun Club, with an immense sigh of relief.

The work was resumed the same day. They proceeded at once to extract the interior mould, clearing out the boring of the piece. Pickaxes and drills were set to work without intermission. The clayey and sandy soils had grown extremely hard under the action of the heat; but the rubbish dug out was rapidly carted away on railway wagons; and such was the ardour of the work, so persuasive the arguments of Barbicane's dollars, that by the 3rd September all traces of the mould had entirely disappeared.

Immediately the operation of boring was commenced; and by the aid of powerful machines, a few weeks later, the inner surface of the immense tube had been made perfectly cylindrical, and the bore of the piece had acquired a thorough polish.

At length, on the 22nd September, less than a twelve-month after Barbicane's original proposal, the enormous weapon, acurately bored, and pointed vertically, was ready for work. There was now only the moon to wait for; and they were pretty sure that she would not fail in the rendezvous.

The ecstasy of J. T. Maston knew no bounds, and he narrowly escaped a frightful fall while staring down the tube. But for the strong hand of Colonel Blomsberry, the worthy secretary, like a modern Erostratus, would have found his death in the depths of the Columbiad.

The cannon was then finished; there was no possible doubt as to its perfect completion. So, on 6th October, Captain Nicholl opened an account between himself and President Barbicane, in which he debited himself to the latter in the sum of 2,000 dollars. One may believe that the Captain's wrath was increased to its highest point, and must have made him seriously ill. However, he still had three bets of three, four, and five thousand dollars respectively; and if he gained two, his position would not be very bad. But the money question did not enter into his calculations; it was the success of his rival in casting a cannon against which iron plates sixty feet thick would have been ineffectual, that dealt him a terrible blow.

After the 23rd September the enclosure of Stones Hill was thrown open to the public; and it will be easily imagined what was the concourse of visitors to this spot! There was an incessant flow of people to and from Tampa Town and the site which resembled a procession, or rather, in fact, a pilgrimage.

It was already clear that, on the day of the experiment itself, the spectators would be counted by millions; for they were already arriving from all parts of the earth upon this narrow promontory. Europe was emigrating to America.

Up to that time, however, it must be confessed, the curiosity of the numerous comers was but scantily gratified. Most had counted upon witnessing the casting, and they were treated to nothing but smoke. This was sorry food for hungry eyes; but Barbicane would admit no one to that operation. Then ensued grumbling, discontent, murmurs; they blamed the President, taxed him with dictatorial conduct. His proceedings were declared "un-American." There was very nearly a riot round Stones Hill; but Barbicane remained inflexible. When, however, the Columbiad was entirely finished, this state of closed doors could no longer be maintained; besides it would have been bad taste, and even imprudence, to affront the public feeling. Barbicane, therefore, opened the enclosure to all comers; but, true to his practical nature, he determined to coin money out of the public curiosity.

It was something, indeed, to be enabled to contemplate this immense Columbiad; but to descend into its depths, this seemed to the Americans the *ne plus ultra* of earthly felicity. Consequently, there was not one curious spectator who was not willing to give himself the treat of visiting the interior of this metallic abyss. Baskets suspended from steam-cranes permitted them to satisfy their curiosity. There was a perfect mania. Women, children, old men, all made it a point of duty to penetrate the mysteries of the colossal gun. The fare for the descent was fixed at five dollars per head; and, despite this high charge, during the two months which preceded the experiment, the influx of visitors enabled the Gun Club to pocket nearly 500,000 dollars!

It is needless to say that the first visitors of the Columbiad were the members of the Gun Club, a privilege justly reserved for that illustrious body. The ceremony took place on the 25th September. A basket of honour took down the President, J. T. Maston, Major Elphinstone, General Morgan, Colonel Blomsberry, and other members of the club, ten in all. How hot it was at the bottom of that long tube of metal! They were half suffocated. But what delight! What ecstasy! A table with six covers had been laid on the massive stone which formed the bottom of the Columbiad, and lighted by a jet of electric light resembling that of day. Numerous exquisite dishes, which seemed to descend from heaven, were placed successively before the guests, and the richest wines of France flowed in profusion during this splendid repast, served nine hundred feet beneath the surface of the earth!

The festival was animated, not to say somewhat noisy. Toasts flew backwards and forwards. They drank to the earth and to her satellite, to the Gun Club, the Union, the moon, Diana, Phœbe, Selene, the "peaceful courier of the night!" All the hurrahs, carried upwards upon the sonorous waves of the immense acoustic tube, arrived at its mouth with the sound of thunder; and the multitude ranged round Stones Hill heartily united their shouts with those of the ten revellers hidden from view at the bottom of the gigantic Columbiad.

J. T. Maston was no longer master of himself. Whether he shouted or gesticulated, ate or drank most, would be a difficult matter to decide. At all events, he would not have given his place up for an empire, "not even if the cannon—loaded, primed, and fired at that very moment—were to blow him in pieces into the planetary world."

## CHAPTER 16

# A TELEGRAM

The great work undertaken by the Gun Club had now virtually come to an end; and two months still remained before the day for the shot to be fired to the moon. To the general impatience these two months appeared as long as years! Hitherto the smallest details of the operation had been daily chronicled by the journals, which the public devoured with eager eyes.

Just at this moment a circumstance, the most unexpected, the most extraordinary and incredible, occurred to rouse afresh their panting spirits, and to throw every mind into a state of the most violent excitement.

One day, the 30th September, at 3.47 p.m., a telegram transmitted by cable from Valentia (Ireland) to Newfoundland and the American mainland, arrived at the address of President Barbicane.

The President tore open the envelope and read the despatch; and, despite his remarkable powers of self-control, his lips turned pale and his eyes grew dim, on reading the twenty words of this telegram.

Here is the text of the despatch, which figures now in the archives of the Gun Club:

"FRANCE, PARIS
"30 *September,* 4 *a.m.*
"Barbicane, Tampa Town, Florida, United States.
"Substitute for your spherical shell a cylindro-conical projectile. I shall go inside. Shall arrive by steamer *Atlanta.*

"MICHEL ARDAN."

## CHAPTER 17

# THE PASSENGER OF THE "ATLANTA"

If this astounding news, instead of flying through the electric wires, had simply arrived by post in the ordinary sealed envelope, Barbicane would not have hesitated a moment. He would have held his tongue about it, both as a measure of prudence, and not to have to reconsider his plans. This telegram might be a cover for some jest, especially as it came from a Frenchman. What human being would ever have conceived the idea of such a journey? and, if such a person really existed, he must be an idiot, whom one would shut up in a lunatic asylum rather than within the walls of the projectile.

The contents of the despatch, however, speedily became known; for the telegraph officials possessed but little discretion, and Michel Ardan's proposal ran at once throughout the several States of the Union. Barbicane had, therefore, no further motive for keeping silence. Consequently, he called together such of his colleagues as were at the moment in Tampa Town, and without expressing his own opinions simply read the laconic text itself. It was received with every possible variety of expressions of doubt, incredulity, and derision from everyone, with the exception of J. T. Maston, who exclaimed, "But it's a grand idea!"

When Barbicane originally proposed to send a shot to the moon everyone looked upon the enterprise as simple and practicable enough—a mere question of gunnery; but when a person, professing to be a reasonable being, offered to take passage within the projectile, the whole thing became a farce, or, in plainer language, *a humbug*.

One question, however, remained. Did such a person exist? This telegram flashed across the depths of the Atlantic, the name of the vessel on board which he was to take his passage, and date assigned for his speedy arrival, all combined to give a certain reality to the proposal. They must get some clearer notion of the matter. Scattered groups of inquirers at length condensed themselves into a compact crowd, which made straight for the residence of President Barbicane.

That worthy was keeping quiet to watch events as they arose. But he had forgotten to take into account the public impatience; and it was with no pleasant countenance that he watched the population of Tampa Town gathering under his windows. The murmurs and shouts below presently obliged him to appear. He came forward, therefore, and on silence being procured, a citizen put the following question to him point-blank: "Is the person mentioned in the telegram, under the name of Michel Ardan, on his way here? Yes or no."

"Gentlemen," replied Barbicane, "I know no more than you do."

"We must know," roared the impatient voices.

"Time will show," the President replied calmly.

"Time has no business to keep the whole country in suspense," replied the orator. "Have you altered the plans of the projectile as the telegram suggests?"

"Not yet, gentlemen; but you are right! We must have better information to go by. The telegram must get it for us."

"To the telegraph!" roared the crowd.

Barbicane descended; and heading the immense assemblage, led the way to the telegraph office. A few minutes later a telegram was despatched to the secretary of the underwriters at Liverpool, requesting answers to the following queries:

"About the ship *Atlanta*—when did she leave Europe? Had she a Frenchman named Michel Ardan on board?"

Two hours afterwards Barbicane received information too exact to leave room for the smallest doubt.

"The steamer *Atlanta* from Liverpool put to sea on the 2nd October, bound for Tampa Town, having on board a Frenchman appearing on the list of passengers as Michel Ardan."

That very evening he wrote to the house of Breadwill and Co., requesting them to suspend the casting of the projectile until further orders. On the 20th October, at 9 a.m., the semaphores of the Bahama Canal signalled a thick smoke on the horizon. Two hours later a large steamer exchanged signals with them. The name of the *Atlanta* flew at once over Tampa Town. At four o'clock the English vessel entered the Bay of Espiritu Santo. At five she crossed the passage of Hillisborough Bay at full steam. At six she cast anchor at Port Tampa. The anchor had scarcely caught the sandy bottom when 500 boats surrounded the *Atlanta*, and the steamer was taken by assault. Barbicane was the first to set foot on deck, and in a voice of which he vainly tried to conceal the emotion, called "Michel Ardan."

"Here!" replied an individual perched on the poop.

Barbicane, with arms crossed, looked fixedly at the passenger of the *Atlanta*.

He was a man of about 42 years of age, of large build, but slightly round-shouldered. His massive head momentarily shook a shock of reddish hair, which resembled a lion's mane. His face was short with a broad forehead, and furnished with a moustache as bristly as a cat's, and little patches of yellowish whisker upon full cheeks. Round, wildish eyes, slightly near-sighted, completed a physiognomy essentially *feline*. His nose was firmly shaped, his mouth particularly sweet in expression, high forehead, intelligent and furrowed with wrinkles like a newly-ploughed field. His body was powerfully developed and firmly fixed upon long legs. Muscular arms, and a general air of decision gave him the appearance of a hardy, jolly companion. He was dressed in a suit of ample size, loose neckerchief, open shirt-collar, disclosing a robust neck; his cuffs, through which appeared a pair of red hands, were invariably unbuttoned.

On the bridge of the steamer, in the midst of the crowd, he bustled to and fro, never still for a moment, "dragging his anchors," as the sailors say, gesticulating, making free with everybody, biting his nails with nervous avidity. He was one of those originals which nature sometimes invents in the freak of a moment, and of which she then breaks the mould.

Amongst other peculiarities, this curiosity gave himself out for a sublime ignoramus, "like Shakespeare," and professed supreme contempt for all scientific men. Those "fellows," as he called them, "are only fit to mark the points, while we play the game." He was, in fact, a thorough Bohemian, adventurous, but not an adventurer; a hair-brained fellow, a kind of Icarus, though possessing relays of wings. For the rest, he was ever in scrapes, ending invariably by falling on his feet, like those little pith figures which they sell as children's toys. In four words, his motto was "I have my opinions," and his ruling passion was the love of the impossible.

Such was the passenger of the *Atlanta*, always excitable, as if boiling under the action of some internal fire by the character of his physical organization. If ever two individuals offered a striking contrast to each other, these were certainly Michel Ardan and the Yankee Barbicane; both, moreover, each in his own way, being equally enterprising and daring.

The scrutiny which the President of the Gun Club was giving to this new arrival was quickly interrupted by the shouts and hurrahs of the crowd. The cries became at last so uproarious, and the popular enthusiasm assumed so personal a form, that Michel Ardan, after having shaken hands some thousands of times, at the imminent risk of leaving his fingers behind him, had at last to make a bolt for his cabin.

Barbicane followed him without uttering a word.

"You are Barbicane, I suppose?" said Michel Ardan in a tone of voice in which he would have addressed a friend of twenty years' standing.

"Yes," replied the President of the G.C.

"All right! how d'ye do, Barbicane? how are you getting on—pretty well? that's right."

"So," said Barbicane, without further preliminary, "you are quite determined to go."

"Quite decided."

"Nothing will stop you?"

"Nothing. Have you modified your projectile according to my telegram?"

"I waited for your arrival. But," asked Barbicane again, "have you carefully reflected?"

"Reflected? have I any time to spare? I find an opportunity of making a trip to the moon, and I mean to profit by it. There is the whole gist of the matter."

Barbicane looked hard at this man who spoke so lightly of his project with such complete absence of anxiety. "But, at least," said he, "you have some plans, some means of carrying your project into execution?"

"Excellent, my dear Barbicane; only permit me to offer one remark: My wish is to tell my story once for all, to everybody, and then to have done with it; then there will be no need for recapitulation. So, if you have no objection, assemble your friends, colleagues, the whole town, all Florida, all America if you like, and to-morrow I shall be ready to explain my plans and answer any objections whatever. You may rest assured I shall wait. Will that suit you?"

"All right," replied Barbicane.

So saying, the president left the cabin and informed the crowd of the proposal of Michel Ardan. His words were received with clappings of hands and shouts of joy. They had removed all difficulties. To-morrow everyone would contemplate this European hero at ease. However, some of the spectators, more infatuated than the rest, would not leave the deck of the *Atlanta*. They passed the night on board. Amongst others J. T. Maston got his hook fixed in the combing of the poop, and it pretty nearly required the capstan to get it out again.

"He is a hero! a hero!" he cried, a theme of which he was never tired of ringing the changes; "and we are only like weak, silly women, compared with this European!"

As to the president, after having suggested to the visitors it was time to retire, he re-entered the passenger's cabin and remained there till the bell of the steamer made it midnight.

But then the two rivals in popularity shook hands heartily, and parted on terms of intimate friendship.

## CHAPTER 18

# A MONSTER MEETING

On the following day Barbicane, fearing that indiscreet questions might be put to Michel Ardan, wanted to limit the number of the audience to a few of the initiated, his own colleagues for instance. He might as well have tried to check the Falls of Niagara! He had therefore, to give up the idea, and to let his new friend run the risks of a public conference.

The place chosen for this monster meeting was a vast plain situated in the rear of the town. In a few hours, thanks to the help of the shipping in port, an immense roofing of canvas was stretched over the parched prairie, and protected it from the burning rays of the sun. There 300,000 people braved the stifling heat for many hours while awaiting the arrival of the Frenchman. Of this crowd of spectators some could both see and hear; some saw badly and heard nothing at all; and some could neither see nor hear anything at all.

At three o'clock Michel Ardan made his appearance, accompanied by the principal members of the Gun Club. He was supported on his right by President Barbicane, and on his left by J. T. Maston, more radiant than the midday sun and nearly as ruddy. Ardan mounted a platform, from the top of which his view extended over a sea of black hats. He exhibited not the slightest embarrassment; he was just as gay, familiar, and pleasant as if he were at home. To the hurrahs which greeted him he replied by a graceful bow; then, waving his hand to request silence, he spoke in perfectly correct English:

"Gentlemen, despite the very hot weather I request your patience for a short time while I offer some explanation regarding the projects which seem to have so deeply interested you. I am neither an orator nor a man of science, and I had no idea of addressing you in public; but my friend Barbicane has told me that you would like to hear me, and I am quite at your service. Listen to me, therefore, with your 600,000 ears, and please to excuse the faults of the speaker.

"Now pray do not forget that you see before you a perfect ignoramus, whose ignorance goes so far that he cannot even understand the difficulties! It seemed to him that it was a matter quite simple, natural, and easy to take one's place in a projectile and start for the moon! That journey must be undertaken sooner or later; and, as for the mode of locomotion adopted, it follows simply the law of progress. Man began by walking on all-fours; then, one fine day, on two feet; then in a carriage, then in a stage-coach; and lastly by railway. Well, the projectile is the vehicle of the future, and the planets themselves are nothing else!

"Now some of you, gentlemen, may imagine that the velocity we propose to impart to it is extravagant. It is nothing of the kind. All the stars exceed it in rapidity, and the earth herself is at this moment carrying us round the sun at three times as rapid a rate, and yet she is a mere lounger on the way compared with many others of the planets! And her velocity is constantly *decreasing*. Is it not evident, then, I ask you, that there will some day appear velocities far greater than these, of which light or electricity will probably be the motive power?

"Yes, gentlemen," continued the orator, "in spite of the opinions of certain narrow-minded people, who would shut up the human race upon this globe, as within some magic circle which it must never outstep, we shall one day travel to the moon, the planets, and the stars, with the same facility, rapidity, and certainty as we now make the voyage from Liverpool to New York! Distance is but a relative expression, and must end by being reduced to zero."

The assembly, strongly predisposed as they were in favour of the French hero, were slightly staggered at this bold theory. Michel Ardan perceived the fact.

"Gentlemen," he continued with a pleasant smile, "you do not seem quite convinced. Very good! Let us reason the matter out. Do you know how long it would take for an *express train* to reach the moon? Three hundred days; no more! And what is that? The distance is no more than nine times the circumference of the earth; and there are no sailors or travellers, of even moderate activity, who have not made longer journeys than that in their lifetime. And now consider that I shall be only ninety-seven hours on my journey.

"Ah! I see you are reckoning that the moon is a long way off from the earth, and that one must think twice before making the experiment. What would you say, then, if we were talking of going to Neptune, which revolves at a distance of more than two thousand seven hundred and twenty millions of miles from the sun! And yet what is that compared with the distance of the fixed stars, some of which, such as Arcturus, are at billions of miles distant from us? And then you talk of the *distance* which separates the planets from the sun! And there are people who affirm that such a thing as distance exists. Absurdity, folly, idiotic nonsense!

"Would you like to know what I think of our own solar universe? Shall I tell you my theory? It is very simple! In my opinion the solar system is a solid, homogeneous body; the planets which compose it are in *actual contact* with each other; and whatever space exists between them is nothing more than the space which separates the molecules of the densest metal, such as silver, iron, or platinum! I have the right, therefore, to affirm, and I repeat, with the conviction which must penetrate all your minds, 'Distance is but an empty name; distance does not really exist!' "

"Hurrah!" cried one voice (need it be said it was that of J. T. Maston?). "Distance does not exist!" And overcome by the energy of his movements, he nearly fell from the platform to the ground. He just escaped a severe fall, which would have proved to him that distance was by no means *an empty name.*

"Gentlemen," resumed the orator, "I repeat that the distance between the earth and her satellite is a mere trifle, and undeserving of serious consideration. I am convinced that before twenty years are over one half of our earth will have paid a visit to the moon. Now, my worthy friends, if you have any question to put to me, you will, I fear, sadly embarrass a poor man like myself; still I will do my best to answer you."

Up to this point the President of the Gun Club had been satisfied with the turn which the discussion had assumed. It became now, however, desirable to divert Ardan from questions of a practical nature, with which he was doubtless far less conversant. Barbicane, therefore, hastened to get in a word, and began by asking his new friend whether he thought that the moon and the planets were inhabited.

"You put before me a great problem, my worthy President," replied the orator, smiling. "Still, men of great intelligence, such as Plutarch, Swedenborg, Bernardin de St. Pierre, and others have, if I mistake not, pronounced in the affirmative. Looking at the question from the natural philosopher's point of view, I should say that *nothing useless* existed in the world; and, replying to your question by another, I should venture to assert, that if these worlds are *habitable*, they either are, have been, or will be inhabited."

"No one could answer more logically or fairly," replied the president. "The question then reverts to this: *Are* these worlds habitable? For my own part I believe they are."

"For myself, I feel certain of it," said Michel Ardan.

"Nevertheless," retorted one of the audience, "there are many arguments *against* the habitability of the worlds. The conditions of life must evidently be greatly modified upon the majority of them. To mention only the planets, we should be either broiled alive in some, or frozen to death in others, according as they are more or less removed from the sun."

"I regret," replied Michel Ardan, "that I have not the honour of personally knowing my contradictor, for I would have attempted to answer him. His objection has its merits, I admit; but I think we may successfully combat it, as well as all others which affect the habitability of the other worlds.

"If I were a *natural philosopher*, I would tell him that if less of caloric were *set in motion* upon the planets which are nearest to the sun, and more, on the contrary, upon those which are farthest removed from it, this simple fact would alone suffice to equalize the heat, and to render the temperature of those worlds supportable by beings organized like ourselves.

"If I were a *naturalist*, I would tell him that, according to some illustrious men of science, nature has furnished us with instances upon the earth of animals existing under very varying conditions of life; that fish respire in a medium fatal to other animals; that amphibious creatures possess a double existence very difficult to explain; that certain denizens of the seas maintain life at enormous depths, and there support a pressure equal to that of fifty or sixty atmospheres without being crushed; that several aquatic insects, regardless of temperature, are met with equally among boiling springs and in the frozen plains of the Polar Sea; in fine, that we cannot help recognizing in nature a diversity of means of operation oftentimes incomprehensible, but not the less real.

"If I were a *chemist*, I would tell him that the meteors, bodies evidently formed outside our terrestrial globe, have, upon analysis, revealed indisputable traces of carbon, a substance which owes its origin solely to organized beings, and which, according to the experiments of Reichenbach, must necessarily itself have been *endued with animation*.

"And lastly, were I a *theologian*, I would tell him that the scheme of the Divine Redemption, according to St. Paul, seems to be applicable, not merely to the earth, but to all the celestial worlds. But, unfortunately I am neither theologian, nor chemist, nor naturalist, nor philosopher; therefore, in my absolute ignorance of the great laws which govern the universe, I confine myself to saying in reply, 'I do not know whether the worlds are inhabited or not; and since I do not know, *I am going to see!*'"

Whether Michel Ardan's antagonist hazarded any further arguments or not it is impossible to say, for the uproarious shouts of the crowd would not let any expression of opinion gain a hearing. On silence being restored, the triumphant orator contented himself with adding the following remarks:

"Gentlemen, you will observe that I have but slightly touched upon this great question. There is another altogether different line of arguments in favour of the habitability of the stars, which I omit for the present. I only desire to call attention to one point. To those who maintain that the planets are *not* inhabited one may reply:

"You might be perfectly in the right, if you could only show that the earth is the *best possible world*, spite of what Voltaire has said. She has but *one* satellite, while Jupiter, Uranus, Saturn, Neptune have several each, an advantage by no means to be despised. But what renders our own globe so uncomfortable is the inclination of its axis to the plane of its orbit. Hence the inequality of days and nights; hence the disagreeable diversity of the season. On the surface of our unhappy spheroid we are always either too hot or too cold; we are frozen in winter, broiled in summer; it is the planet of rheumatism, coughs, bronchitis; while on the surface of Jupiter, for example, where the axis is but slightly inclined, the inhabitants may enjoy uniform temperatures. It possesses zones of perpetual springs, summers, autumns, and winters; every Jovian may choose for himself what climate he likes, and there spend the whole of his life in security from all variations of temperature. You will, I am sure, readily admit this superiority of Jupiter over our own planet, to say nothing of his years, which equal twelve of ours! Under such auspices, and such marvellous conditions of existence, it appears to me that the inhabitants of so fortunate a world must be in every respect superior to ourselves. All we require, in order to attain to such perfection, is the mere trifle of having an axis of rotation less inclined to the plane of its orbit!"

"Hurrah!" roared an energetic voice, "let us unite our efforts, invent the necessary machines, and rectify the earth's axis!"

A thunder of applause followed this proposal, the author of which was, of course, no other than J. T. Maston. And, in all probability, if the truth must be told, if the Yankees could only have found a point of application for it, they would have constructed a lever capable of raising the earth and rectifying its axis. It was just this deficiency which baffled these daring mechanicians.

## CHAPTER 19

# ATTACK AND RIPOSTE

As soon as the excitement had subsided, the following words were heard in a strong and determined voice:

"Now that the speaker has favoured us with so much imagination, would he be so good as to return to his subject, and give us a little practical view of the question?"

All eyes were directed towards the person who spoke. He was a little dried-up man, of an active figure, with an American "goatee" beard. Profiting by the different movements in the crowd, he had managed by degrees to gain the front row of the spectators. There, with arms crossed and stern gaze, he watched the hero of the meeting. After having put his question he remained silent, and appeared to take no notice of the thousands of looks directed towards himself, nor of the murmur of disapprobation excited by his words. Meeting at first with no reply, he repeated his question with marked emphasis, adding, "We are here to talk about the *moon* and not about the *earth*."

"You are right, sir," replied Michel Ardan; "the discussion has become irregular. We will return to the moon."

"Sir," said the unknown, "you maintain that our satellite is inhabited. Very good; but if Selenites do exist, that race of beings assuredly must live without breathing, for—I warn you for your own sake—there is not the smallest particle of air on the surface of the moon."

At this remark Ardan pushed up his shock of red hair; he saw that he was on the point of being involved in a struggle with this person upon the very gist of the whole question. He looked sternly at him in his turn and said:

"Oh! so there is no air in the moon? And pray, if you are so good, who ventures to affirm that?"

"The men of science."

"Really?"

"Really."

"Sir," replied Michel, "joking apart, I have a profound respect for men of science who do possess science, but a profound contempt for men of science who do not."

"Do you know any who belong to the latter category?"

"Decidedly. In France there are some who maintain that, mathematically, a bird cannot possibly fly; and others who demonstrate theoretically that fishes were never made to live in water."

"I have nothing to do with persons of that description, and I can quote, in support of my statement, names which you cannot refuse deference to."

"Then, sir, you will sadly embarrass a poor ignoramus, who, besides, asks nothing better than to learn."

"Why, then, do you introduce scientific questions if you have never studied them?" asked the unknown somewhat coarsely.

"For the reason that 'he is always brave who never suspects danger.' I know nothing, it is true; but it is precisely my very weakness which constitutes my strength."

"Your weakness amounts to folly," retorted the unknown in a passion.

"All the better," replied our Frenchman, "if it carries me up to the *moon*."

Barbicane and his colleagues devoured with their eyes the intruder who had so boldly placed himself in antagonism to their enterprise. Nobody knew him, and the president, uneasy as to the result of so free a discussion, watched his new friend with some anxiety. The meeting began to be somewhat fidgety also, for the contest directed their attention to the dangers, if not the actual impossibilities, of the proposed expedition.

"Sir," replied Ardan's antagonist, "there are many and incontrovertible reasons which prove the absence of an atmosphere in the moon. I might say that, *a priori*, if one ever did exist, it must have been absorbed by the earth; but I prefer to bring forward indisputable facts."

"Bring them forward then, sir, as many as you please."

"You know," said the stranger, "that when any luminous rays cross a medium such as air, they are deflected out of the straight line; in other words, they undergo *refraction*. Well! When stars are occulted by the moon, their rays, on grazing the edge of her disc, exhibit not the least deviation, nor offer the slightest indication of refraction. It follows, therefore, that the moon cannot be surrounded by an atmosphere."

"In point of fact," replied Ardan, "this is your chief, if not your *only* argument; and a really scientific man might be puzzled to answer it. For myself, I will simply say that it is defective, because it assumes that the angular diameter of the moon has been completely determined, which is not the case. But let us proceed. Tell me, my dear sir, do you admit the existence of volcanoes on the moon's surface?"

"*Extinct*, yes! In activity, no."

"These volcanoes, however, were at one time in a state of activity?"

"True! but, as they themselves supplied the oxygen they needed for combustion, the mere fact of their eruption does not prove the presence of an atmosphere."

"Proceed again, then; and let us set aside this class of arguments in order to come to direct observations. In 1715 the astronomers Louville and Halley, watching the eclipse of the 3rd May, remarked some very extraordinary scintillations. These jets of light, rapid in nature, and of frequent recurrence, they attributed to thunderstorms in the lunar atmosphere."

"In 1715," replied the unknown, "the astronomers Louville and Halley mistook for lunar phenomena some which were purely terrestrial, such as meteoric or other bodies which appear in our own atmosphere. This was the scientific explanation at the time of the facts; and that is my answer now."

"On again, then," replied Ardan; "Herschel, in 1787, observed a great number of luminous points on the moon's surface, did he not?"

"Yes! but without offering any solution of them. Herschel himself never inferred the necessity of a lunar atmosphere. And I may add that Baer and Maedler, the two great authorities upon the moon, are quite agreed as to the entire absence of air on its surface."

A movement was here manifest among the assemblage, who appeared to be growing excited by the arguments of this singular personage.

"Let us proceed," replied Ardan, with perfect coolness, "and come to one important fact. A skilful French astronomer, M. Laussedat, in watching the eclipse of 18th July, 1860, proved that the horns of the solar crescent were *rounded and truncated*. Now, this appearance could only have been produced by a deviation of the solar rays in traversing the atmosphere of the moon. There is no other possible explanation of the fact."

"But is this established as a fact?"

"Absolutely certain."

A counter-movement here took place in favour of the hero of the meeting, whose opponent was now reduced to silence. Ardan resumed the conversation; and, without exhibiting any exultation at the advantage he had gained, simply said:

"You see, then, my dear sir, we must not pronounce with absolute positiveness against the existence of an atmosphere in the moon. That atmosphere is, probably, of extreme rarity; nevertheless at the present day science generally admits that it exists."

"Not in the mountains, at all events," returned the unknown, unwilling to give in.

"No! but at the bottom of the valleys, and not exceeding a few hundred feet in height."

"In any case you will do well to take every precaution, for the air will be terribly rarefied."

"My good sir, there will always be enough for a solitary individual; besides, once arrived up there, I shall do my best to economize, and not to breath except on grand occasions!"

A tremendous roar of laughter rang in the ears of the mysterious interlocutor, who glared fiercely round upon the assembly.

"Then," continued Ardan, with a careless air, "since we are in accord regarding the presence of a certain atmosphere, we are forced to admit the presence of a certain quantity of water. This is a happy consequence for me. Moreover, my amiable contradictor, permit me to submit one further observation. We only know *one* side of the moon's disc; and if there is but little air on the face presented to us, it is possible that there is plenty on the one turned away from us."

"And for what reason?"

"Because the moon, under the action of the earth's attraction, has assumed the form of an egg, which we look at from the smaller end. Hence it follows, by Hausen's calculations, that its centre of gravity is situated in the other hemisphere. Hence it results that the great mass of air and water must have been drawn away to the other face of our satellite during the first days of its creation."

"Pure fancies!" cried the unknown.

"No! Pure theories! which are based upon the laws of mechanics, and it seems difficult for me to refute them. I appeal then to this meeting, and I put it to them whether life, such as exists upon the earth, is possible on the surface of the moon?"

Three hundred thousand auditors at once applauded the proposition. Ardan's opponent tried to get in another word, but he could not obtain a hearing. Cries and menaces fell upon him like hail.

"Enough! enough!" cried some.

"Drive the intruder off!" shouted others.

"Turn him out!" roared the exasperated crowd.

But he, holding firmly on to the platform, did not budge an inch, and let the storm pass over him. It which would soon have assumed formidable proportions, if Michel Ardan had not quieted it by a gesture. He was too chivalrous to abandon his opponent in an apparent extremity.

"You wish to say a few more words?" he asked, in a pleasant voice.

"Yes, a thousand; or rather, no, only one! If you persevere in your enterprise, you must be a——"

"Very rash person! How can you treat me as such? me, who have demanded a cylindroconical projectile, in order to prevent turning round and round on my way like a squirrel?"

"But, unhappy man, the dreadful shock will smash you to pieces at the outset."

"My dear contradictor, you have just put your finger upon the true and the only difficulty; nevertheless, I have too good an opinion of the industrial genius of the Americans not to believe that they will succeed in overcoming it."

"But the heat developed by the rapidity of the projectile in traversing the air?"

"Oh! the walls are thick, and I shall soon have crossed the atmosphere."

"But victuals and water?"

"I have calculated for a twelvemonth's supply, and I shall be only four days on the journey."

"But for air to breathe on the journey?"

"I shall make it by a chemical process."

"But your fall on the moon, supposing you ever reach it?"

"It will be six times less dangerous than a sudden fall upon the earth, because the weight will be only one-sixth as great on the surface of the moon."

"Still, it will be enough to smash you like glass!"

"What is to prevent my retarding the shock by means of rockets conveniently placed, and lighted at the right moment?"

"But after all, supposing all difficulties surmounted, all obstacles removed, supposing everything combined to favour you, and granting that you may arrive safe and sound in the moon, how will you come back?"

"I am not coming back!"

At this reply, almost sublime in its very simplicity, the assembly became silent. But its silence was more eloquent than could have been its cries of enthusiasm. The unknown profited by the opportunity and once more protested:

"You will inevitably kill yourself!" he cried; "and your death will be that of a madman, useless even to science!"

"Go on, my dear unknown, for truly your prophecies are most agreeable!"

"It really is too much!" cried Michel Ardan's adversary. "I do not know why I should continue so frivolous a discussion! Please yourself about this insane expedition! We need not trouble ourselves about *you!*"

"Pray don't stand upon ceremony!"

"No! another person is responsible for your act."

"Who, may I ask?" demanded Michel Ardan in an imperious tone.

"The ignoramus who organized this absurd and impossible experiment!"

The attack was direct. Barbicane, ever since the inter-
ference of the unknown, had been making fearful efforts at
self-control; now, however, seeing himself directly attacked,
he could restrain himself no longer. He rose suddenly, and
was rushing upon the enemy who thus braved him to the
face, when all at once he found himself separated from him.

The platform was lifted by a hundred strong arms, and
the President of the Gun Club shared triumphal honours
with Michel Ardan. The shield was heavy, but the bearers
came in continuous relays, disputing, struggling, even fighting among themselves in their eagerness to lend their shoulders to this demonstration.

However, the unknown had not profited by the tumult
to quit his post. Besides, he could not have done it in the
midst of that compact crowd. There he held on in the front
row, with crossed arms, glaring at President Barbicane.

The shouts of the immense crowd continued at their
highest pitch throughout this triumphant march. Michel
Ardan took it all with evident pleasure. His face gleamed
with delight. Several times the platform seemed seized with
pitching and rolling like a weather-beaten ship. But the
two heroes of the meeting had good sea-legs. They never
stumbled; and their vessel arrived without dues at the port
of Tampa Town.

Michel Ardan managed, fortunately, to escape from the
last embraces of his vigorous admirers. He made for the
Hotel Franklin, quickly gained his chamber, and slid under
the bed-clothes, while an army of a hundred thousand men
kept watch under his windows.

During this time a scene, short, grave, and decisive, took
place between the mysterious personage and the President
of the Gun Club.

Barbicane, free at last, had gone straight at his adversary.

"Come!" he said shortly.

The other followed him on to the quay; and the two presently found themselves alone at the entrance of an open
wharf on Jones' Fall.

The two enemies, still mutually unknown, gazed at each
other.

"Who are you?" asked Barbicane.

"Captain Nicholl!"

"So I suspected. Hitherto chance has never thrown you in my way."

"I am come for that purpose."

"You have insulted me!"

"Publicly!"

"And you will answer to me for this insult?"

"At this very moment."

"No! I desire that all that passes between us shall be secret. There is a wood situated three miles from Tampa, the wood of Skersnaw. Do you know it?"

"I know it."

"Will you be so good as to enter it to-morrow morning at five o'clock, on one side?"

"Yes! if you will enter at the other side at the same hour."

"And you will not forget your rifle?" said Barbicane.

"No more than you will forget yours," replied Nicholl.

These words having been coldly spoken, the President of the Gun Club and the captain parted. Barbicane returned to his lodging; but, instead of snatching a few hours of repose, he passed the night in endeavouring to discover a method of overcoming the shock of the discharge and solving the difficult problem raised by Michel Ardan during the discussion.

## CHAPTER 20

# HOW A FRENCHMAN MANAGES AN AFFAIR

While the terms of this duel were discussed by the president and the captain—this dreadful, savage duel, in which each adversary became a man-hunter—Michel Ardan was resting from the fatigues of his triumph. *Resting* is hardly an appropriate expression, for American beds rival marble or granite tables for hardness.

Ardan was sleeping, then, badly enough, tossing about between the cloths which served him for sheets, and he was dreaming of making a more comfortable couch in his projectile when a frightful noise disturbed his dreams. Thundering blows shook his door. They seemed to be caused by some iron instrument. A great deal of loud talking was distinguishable in this racket, which was rather too early in the morning. "Open the door," someone shrieked, "for Heaven's sake!"

Ardan saw no reason for complying with a demand so roughly expressed. However, he got up and opened the door just as it was giving way before the blows of this determined visitor. The secretary of the Gun Club burst into the room. A bomb could not have made more noise or have entered the room with less ceremony.

"Last night," cried J. T. Maston, *ex abrupto*, "our president was publicly insulted during the meeting. He challenged his adversary, who is none other than Captain Nicholl! They are fighting this morning in the wood of Skersnaw. I heard all particulars from the mouth of Barbicane himself. If he is killed, then our scheme is at an end. We must prevent this duel, and one man alone has enough influence over Barbicane to stop him, and that man is Michel Ardan."

While J. T. Maston was speaking, Michel Ardan, without interrupting him, had hastily put on his clothes; and, in less than two minutes, the two friends were making for the suburbs of Tampa Town with rapid strides.

It was during this walk that Maston explained the position. He told Ardan the real cause of the hostility between Barbicane and Nicholl; how it was of old standing, and why, thanks to unknown friends, the president and the captain had, as yet, never met face to face. He added that it arose simply from a rivalry between iron plates and shot, and, finally, that the scene at the meeting was only the long-wished-for opportunity for Nicholl to pay off an old grudge.

Nothing is more dreadful than private duels in America. The two adversaries attack each other like wild beasts. Then it is that they might well covet those wonderful powers of the Indians of the prairies—their quick intelligence, their ingenious cunning, their scent of the enemy. A single mistake, a moment's hesitation, a single false step may cause death. On these occasions Yankees are often accompanied by their dogs, and keep up the struggle for hours.

"What demons you are!" cried Michel Ardan, when his companion had depicted this scene to him with much energy.

"Yes we are," replied J. T. modestly; "but we had better make haste."

Though Michel Ardan and he had crossed the plain still wet with dew, and had taken the shortest route over creeks and rice-fields, they could not reach Skersnaw under five hours and a half.

Barbicane must have passed the border half an hour ago.

There was an old woodman working there, occupied in selling faggots from trees that had been levelled by his axe.

Maston ran towards him, saying, "Have you seen a man go into the wood, armed with a rifle? Barbicane, the president, my best friend?"

The worthy secretary of the Gun Club thought that his president must be known by all the world. But the bushman did not seem to understand him.

"A hunter?" said Ardan.

"A hunter? Yes," replied the bushman.

"Long ago?"

"About an hour."

"Too late!" cried Maston.

"Have you heard any shots?" asked Ardan.

"No!"

"Not one?"

"Not one! That hunter did not look as if he knew how to hunt!"

"What is to be done?" said Maston.

"We must go into the wood, at the risk of getting a ball which is not meant for us."

"Ah!" cried Maston, in a tone which could not be mistaken, "I would rather have twenty balls in my own head than one in Barbicane's."

"Forward, then," said Ardan, pressing his companion's hand.

A few moments later the two friends had disappeared in the copse. It was a dense thicket, in which rose huge cypresses, sycamores, tulip-trees, olives, tamarinds, oaks and magnolias. These different trees had interwoven their branches into an inextricable maze, through which the eye could not penetrate.

Michel Ardan and Maston walked side by side in silence through the tall grass, cutting themselves a path through the strong creepers, casting anxious glances on the bushes and every moment expecting to hear the sound of rifles. As for the traces which Barbicane ought to have left of his passage through the wood, there was not a vestige of them: so they followed the barely perceptible paths along which Indians had tracked their enemy, and which the dense foliage darkly overshadowed.

After an hour spent in vain pursuit the two stopped, in intensified anxiety.

"It must be all over," said Maston, discouraged. "A man like Barbicane would not dodge his enemy, or ensnare him, would not even manœuvre! He is too open, too brave. He has gone straight ahead, right into the danger, and doubtless far enough from the woodman for the wind to prevent his hearing the report of the rifles."

"But surely," replied Michel Ardan, "since we entered the wood we should have heard!"

"And what if we came too late?" cried Maston in tones of despair.

For once Ardan had no reply to make, he and Maston resuming their walk in silence. From time to time, indeed, they raised great shouts, alternately calling Barbicane and Nicholl, neither of whom, however, answered their cries. Only the birds, awakened by the sound, flew past them and disappeared among the branches, while some frightened deer fled precipitately before them.

For another hour their search was continued. The greater part of the wood had been explored. There was nothing to reveal the presence of the combatants. The information the woodman had given them was after all doubtful, and Ardan was about to propose abandoning this useless pursuit, when all at once Maston stopped.

"Hush!" said he, "there is someone down there!"

"Someone?" repeated Michel Ardan.

"Yes; a man! He seems motionless. His rifle is not in his hands. What can he be doing?"

"But can you recognize him?" asked Ardan, whose short sight was little use to him in such circumstances.

"Yes! Yes! He is turning towards us," answered Maston.

"And it is?"

"Captain Nicholl!"

"Nicholl?" cried Michel Ardan, feeling a terrible pang of grief.

"Nicholl unarmed! So he doesn't fear his adversary any longer!"

"Let's go to him," said Michel Ardan, "and find out the truth."

But he and his companion had barely taken fifty steps when they paused to examine the captain more attentively. They expected to find a bloodthirsty man, happy in his revenge!

On seeing him, they paused, stupefied.

A net, composed of very fine meshes, hung between two enormous tulip-trees, and in the midst of this snare, with its wings entangled, was a poor little bird, uttering pitiful cries, while it vainly struggled to escape. The bird-catcher who had laid this snare was no human being, but a venomous spider, peculiar to that country, as large as a pigeon's egg, and armed with enormous claws. The hideous creature, instead of rushing on its prey, had beaten a sudden retreat and taken refuge in the upper branches of the tulip-tree, for a formidable enemy menaced its stronghold.

Here, then, was Nicholl, his gun on the ground, forgetful of danger, trying if possible to save the victim from its cobweb prison. At last it was accomplished, and the little bird flew joyfully away and disappeared.

Nicholl lovingly watched its flight, when he heard these words pronounced by a voice full of emotion:

"You are indeed a brave man!"

He turned. Michel Ardan was before him, repeating in a different tone:

"And a kindhearted one!"

"Michel Ardan!" cried the captain. "Why are you here?"

"To press your hand, Nicholl, and to prevent you from either killing Barbicane or being killed by him."

"Barbicane!" returned the captain. "I have been looking for him for the last two hours in vain. Where is he hiding?"

"Nicholl!" said Michel Ardan, "this is not courteous! we ought always to treat an adversary with respect; rest assured if Barbicane is still alive we shall find him all the more easily; because if he has not, like you, been amusing himself with freeing oppressed birds, he must be looking for you. When we have found him, Michel Ardan tells you this, there will be no duel between you."

"Between President Barbicane and myself," gravely replied Nicholl, "there is rivalry which the death of one of us——"

"Pooh, pooh!" said Ardan. "Brave fellows like you indeed! you shall not fight!"

"I will fight, sir!"

"No!"

"Captain," said J. T. Maston, with much feeling, "I am a friend of the president's, his *alter ego*, his second self; if you really must kill someone, *shoot me*! it will do just as well!"

"Sir," Nicholl replied, seizing his rifle convulsively, "these jokes——"

"Our friend Maston is not joking," replied Ardan. "I fully understand his idea of being killed himself in order to save his friend. But neither he nor Barbicane will fall before the balls of Captain Nicholl. Indeed I have so attractive a proposal to make to the two rivals, that both will be eager to accept it."

"What is it?" asked Nicholl with manifest incredulity.

"Patience!" exclaimed Ardan. "I can only reveal it in the presence of Barbicane."

"Let us go in search of him then!" cried the captain.

The three men started off at once; having unloaded his rifle, the captain shouldered it and went forward in silence.

Another half an hour passed, and the pursuit was still fruitless. Maston was oppressed by sinister forebodings. He looked fiercely at Nicholl, asking himself whether the captain's vengeance had been already satisfied, and the unfortunate Barbicane, shot, was perhaps lying dead on some bloodstained path. The same thought seemed to occur to Ardan; and both were casting inquiring glances on Nicholl, when suddenly Maston paused.

The motionless figure of a man leaning against a gigantic catalpa appeared twenty feet off, half veiled by the foliage.

"It is he!" said Maston.

Barbicane never moved. Ardan looked at the captain, but he did not wince. Ardan went forward crying:

"Barbicane, Barbicane!"

No answer! Arden rushed towards his friend; but in the act of seizing his arms, he stopped short and uttered a cry of surprise.

Barbicane, pencil in hand, was tracing geometrical figures in a memorandum book, whilst his unloaded rifle lay beside him on the ground.

Absorbed in his studies, Barbicane, in his turn forgetful of the duel, had seen and heard nothing.

When Ardan took his hand, he looked up and stared at his visitors in astonishment.

"Ah, it is you!" he cried at last. "I have found it, my friend, I have found it!"

"What?"

"My plan!"

"What plan?"

"The plan for counteracting the effect of the shock of the explosion!"

Indeed?" said Michel Ardan, looking at the captain out of the corner of his eye.

"Yes! water! simply water, which will act as a spring—ah! Maston," cried Barbicane, "you here also?"

"Himself," replied Ardan; "and permit me to introduce to you at the same time the worthy Captain Nicholl!"

"Nicholl!" cried Barbicane, who jumped up at once. "Pardon me, captain, I had quite forgotten—I am ready!"

Michel Ardan interfered, without giving the two enemies time to say anything more.

"Thank Heaven!" said he. "It is a happy thing that brave men like you two did not meet sooner! We should now have been mourning for one or other of you. But, thanks to Providence, which has interfered, there is now no further cause for alarm. When one forgets one's anger in mechanics or in cobwebs, it is a sign that the anger is not dangerous."

Michel Ardan then told the president how the captain had been found occupied.

"I put it to you now," said he in conclusion, "are two such good fellows as you are made on purpose to smash each other's skulls with shot?"

There was in "the situation" somewhat of the ridiculous, something quite unexpected: Michel Ardan saw this, and determined to effect a reconciliation.

"My good friends," said he, with his most bewitching smile, "this is nothing but a misunderstanding. Nothing more! well! to prove that it is all over between you, accept frankly the proposal I am going to make to you."

"Make it," said Nicholl.

"Our friend Barbicane believes that his projectile will go straight to the moon?"

"Yes, certainly," replied the president.

"And our friend Nicholl is persuaded it will fall back upon the earth?"

"I am certain of it," cried the captain.

"Good!" said Ardan. "I cannot pretend to make you agree; but I suggest this: Go with me, and so see whether we are stopped on our journey."

"What?" exclaimed J. T. Maston, stupefied.

The two rivals, on this sudden proposal, looked steadily

at each other. Barbicane waited for the captain's answer. Nicholl watched for the decision of the president.

"Well?" said Michel. "There is now no fear of the shock!"

"Done!" cried Barbicane.

But quickly as he pronounced the word, he was not before Nicholl.

"Hurrah! bravo! hip! hip! hurrah!" cried Michel, giving a hand to each of the late adversaries. "Now that it is all settled, my friends, allow me to treat you after the French fashion. Let's have breakfast!"

## CHAPTER 21

# THE NEW CITIZEN OF
# THE UNITED STATES

That same day all America heard of the affair of Captain Nicholl and President Barbicane, as well as its singular *denouement*. From that day forth, Michel Ardan had not one moment's rest. Deputations from all corners of the Union harrassed him without cessation or intermission. He was compelled to receive them all, whether he would or no. How many hands he shook, how many people he was "hail-fellow-well-met" with, it is impossible to guess! Such a triumphal result would have intoxicated any other man; but he managed to keep himself in a state of delightful *semi*-tipsiness.

Among the deputations of all kinds which assailed him, that of "The Lunatics" were careful not to forget what they owed to the future conqueror of the moon. One day, certain of these poor people, so numerous in America, came to call upon him, and requested permission to return with him to their native country.

"Singular hallucinations!" said he to Barbicane, after having dismissed the deputation with promises to convey numbers of messages to friends in the moon. "Do you believe in the influence of the moon upon disease?"

"Scarcely!"

"No more do I, despite some remarkable recorded facts of history. For instance, during an epidemic in 1693, a large number of persons died at the very moment of an eclipse. The celebrated Bacon always fainted during an eclipse. Charles VI relapsed six times into madness during the year 1399, sometimes during the new, sometimes during the full moon. Gall observed that insane persons underwent an accession of their disorder twice in every month, at the epochs of new and full moon. In fact, numerous observations made upon fevers, somnambulisms, and other human maladies, seem to prove that the moon does exercise some mysterious influence upon man."

"But the why and the wherefore?" asked Barbicane.

"Well, I can only give you the answer which Arago borrowed from Plutarch, which is nineteen centuries old. 'Perhaps the stories are not true!'"

In the height of his triumph, Michel Ardan had to encounter all the annoyances incidental to a man of celebrity. Managers of entertainments wanted to exhibit him. Barnum offered him a million dollars to make the tour of the United States in his show. As for his photographs, they were sold in all sizes, and his portrait taken in every imaginable posture. More than half a million copies were disposed of in an incredibly short space of time.

But it was not only the men who paid him homage, but the women also. He might have married well a hundred times over, if he had been willing to settle in life. The old maids, in particular, of forty years and upwards, and dry in proportion, devoured his photographs day and night. They would have married him by hundreds, even if he had imposed upon them the condition of accompanying him into space. He had, however, no intention of transplanting a race of Franco-Americans upon the surface of the moon.

He therefore declined all offers.

As soon as he could withdraw from these somewhat embarrassing demonstrations, he went, accompanied by his friends, to pay a visit to the Columbiad. He was highly gratified by his inspection, and made the descent to the bottom of the tube of this gigantic gun, which was presently to launch him to the moon.

Here must be mentioned a proposal of J. T. Maston's. When the secretary of the Gun Club found that Barbicane and Nicholl accepted the proposal of Michel Ardan, he made up his mind to join them, and make one of a snug party of four. So one day he demanded to be admitted as one of the travellers. Barbicane, pained at having to refuse him, gave him clearly to understand that the projectile could not possibly contain so many passengers. Maston, in despair, went in search of Michel Ardan, who counselled him to resign himself to the situation, adding one or two arguments *ad hominem.*

"You see, old fellow," he said, "you must not take what I say in bad part; but really, between ourselves, you are in too incomplete a condition to appear in the moon!"

"Incomplete?" shrieked the valiant invalid.

"Yes, my dear fellow! Imagine our meeting some of the inhabitants up there! Would you like to give them such a melancholy notion of what goes on down here? to teach them what war is, to inform them that we employ our time chiefly in devouring each other, in smashing arms and legs, and that too on a globe which can support a hundred billions of inhabitants, and which actually does contain nearly two hundred millions? Why, my worthy friend, we should have to turn you out of doors!"

"But still, if you arrive there in pieces, you will be as *incomplete* as I am."

"Unquestionably," replied Michel Ardan; "but we shall not."

In fact, a preparatory experiment, tried on the 18th October, had yielded the best results and caused the most well-grounded hopes of success. Barbicane, anxious to obtain some notion of the effect of the shock at the projectile's departure, had procured a 38-inch mortar from the arsenal of Pensacola. He had this placed on the bank of Hillisborough Roads, so that the shell might drop back into the sea, and the shock of its fall be minimized. His object was to ascertain the extent of the shock of departure, and not that of the return.

A hollow projectile had been prepared for this strange experiment. A thick padding fastened upon a kind of elastic network, made of the best steel, lined the inside of the walls. It was a veritable *nest* most carefully wadded.

"What a pity I can't find room in there," said J. T. Maston, regretting that his height did not allow him to try the adventure.

Within this shell were shut up a large cat, and a squirrel belonging to J. T. Maston, and of which he was particularly fond. They wanted, however, to ascertain how this little animal, least of all others subject to giddiness, would endure this experiment.

The mortar was charged with 160 lb. of powder, and loaded with the shell. On being fired, the projectile rose with great velocity, described a majestic parabola, attained a height of about a thousand feet, and descended in a graceful curve into the midst of the vessels that lay there at anchor.

Without a moment's loss of time a small boat put off in the direction of its fall; some active divers plunged into the water and attached ropes to the handles of the shell, which was quickly dragged on board. Five minutes did not elapse between the moment of enclosing the animals and that of unscrewing the lid of their prison.

Ardan, Barbicane, Maston and Nicholl were present on board the boat, and assisted at the operation with an interest which may readily be comprehended. Hardly had the shell been opened when the cat leaped out, slightly bruised, but full of life, and exhibiting no signs whatever of having made an aerial expedition. No trace, however, of the squirrel could be discovered. The truth at last became apparent —the cat had eaten its fellow-traveller!

J. T. Maston grieved much for the loss of his poor squirrel and proposed to add its fate to that of other martyrs to science.

After this experiment all hesitation, all fear disappeared. Besides, Barbicane's plans would ensure greater perfection for his projectile and go far to overcome the effects of the shock altogether. Nothing now remained but to go!

Two days later Michel Ardan received a message from the President of the United States, an honour of which he showed himself especially appreciative.

After the example of his illustrious fellow-countrymen, the Marquis de la Fayette, the Government had bestowed upon him the title of "Citizen of the United States of America."

## CHAPTER 22

# THE PROJECTILE

On the completion of the Columbiad the public interest centred in the projectile itself, the vehicle which was destined to carry the three hardy adventurers into space.

The new plans had been sent to Breadwill and Co., of Albany, with the request for their speedy execution. The projectile was consequently cast on the 2nd November, and immediately forwarded by the Eastern Railway to Stones Hill. It arrived without accident on the 10th of that month, when Michel Ardan, Barbicane, and Nicholl were waiting impatiently for it.

The projectile had now to be filled to the depth of three feet with water, intended to support a watertight wooden disc, which moved easily within the walls of the projectile. It was upon this raft that the travellers were to take their place. This volume of water was divided by horizontal partitions, which the shock of the discharge would have to break in succession. Then each sheet of the water, from the lowest to the highest, running off into escape tubes towards the top of the projectile, would form a sort of spring; and the wooden disc, supplied with extremely powerful plugs, could not strike the lowest plate except after successively breaking the different partitions.

Undoubtedly the travellers would still have to encounter a violent impact after the complete escape of the water; but the first shock would be almost entirely destroyed by this powerful spring. The upper part of the walls were lined with a thick padding of leather, fastened upon springs of the best steel, behind which the escape tubes were completely concealed; thus all imaginable precautions had been taken for averting the first shock; and if they *did* get crushed, they must, as Michel Ardan said, be made of very bad material.

The entrance into this metallic tower was by a narrow

aperture in the wall of the cone. This was hermetically closed by an aluminium plate, fastened internally by powerful screw-pressure. The travellers could therefore quit their prison at pleasure, as soon as they reached the moon.

Light and view were given by means of four thick lenticular glass scuttles, two pierced in the circular wall itself, the third in the bottom, the fourth in the top. These scuttles were protected against the shock of departure by plates let into solid grooves, which could easily be opened outwards by unscrewing them from the inside. Reservoirs firmly fixed contained water and the necessary provisions; and fire and light were procurable by means of gas, contained in a special reservoir under a pressure of several atmospheres. They had only to turn a tap, and for six hours the gas would light and warm this comfortable vehicle.

There now remained only the question of air; for allowing for its consumption by Barbicane, his two companions, and two dogs which he meant to take with him, it was necessary to renew the air of the projectile. Now air consists principally of twenty-one parts of oxygen and seventy-nine of nitrogen. The lungs absorb the oxygen, which is indispensable for the support of life, and reject the nitrogen. The air expired loses nearly five per cent. of the former and contains nearly an equal volume of carbon dioxide, produced by the combustion of the elements of the blood. In an airtight enclosure, then, after a certain time, all the oxygen of the air will be replaced by the carbon dioxide—a gas fatal to life.

There were two things to be done then—first, to replace the absorbed oxygen; secondly, to destroy the expired carbonic acid; both easy enough to do, by potassium chlorate and caustic potash. The former is a salt which appears as white crystals; when raised to a temperature of 400° it is transformed into chloride of potassium, and the oxygen which it contains is entirely liberated. Now twenty-eight pounds of chlorate produce seven pounds of oxygen, or 2,400 *litres*—the quantity necessary for the travellers during twenty-four hours.

Caustic potash has a great affinity for carbon dioxide; and it is enough to shake it for it to seize upon the gas and form potassium bicarbonate. By these two means they could be enabled to restore its life-supporting properties to the vitiated air.

It is necessary, however, to add that the experiments had hitherto been made *in anima vili.* Whatever its scientific accuracy was, they did not as yet know how it would answer with human beings. The honour of putting it to the proof was energetically claimed by J. T. Maston.

"Since I am not to go," said the brave artillerist, "I may at least live for a week in the projectile."

It would have been hard to refuse him; so they consented to his wish. A sufficient quantity of potassium chlorate and of caustic potash was placed at his disposal, together with provisions for eight days. And having shaken hands with his friends, on the 12th November, at six a.m., after strictly warning them not to open his prison before the 20th, at six p.m., he slid down into the projectile, the plate of which was at once hermetically sealed.

What did he do with himself during that week? They could get no information. The thickness of the walls of the projectile prevented any sound from reaching from within to the outside. On the 20th November, at six p.m., exactly, the plate was opened.

The friends of J. T. Maston had been all along in a state of much anxiety; but they were promptly reassured on hearing a jolly voice shouting a boisterous hurrah.

Presently the secretary of the Gun Club appeared at the top of the cone in a triumphant attitude. He had grown fat!

## CHAPTER 23

# THE TELESCOPE OF THE ROCKY MOUNTAINS

On the 20th October in the preceding year, after the close of the subscription, the President of the Gun Club had credited the Observatory of Cambridge with the sums necessary for the construction of a gigantic optical instrument. It was designed to render visible on the surface of the moon any object exceeding nine feet in diameter.

At the period when the Gun Club essayed their great experiment, such instruments had reached a high degree of perfection, and produced some magnificent results. Two had remarkable power and gigantic dimensions.

Still, despite these colossal dimensions, the actual enlargement scarcely exceeded 6,000 times; consequently, the moon was brought within no nearer an apparent distance than thirty-nine miles; and objects of less than sixty feet in diameter, unless they were of very considerable length, were still imperceptible.

In dealing with a projectile nine feet in diameter and fifteen feet long, it became necessary to bring the moon within an apparent distance of five miles at most; to obtain a magnifying power of 48,000 times.

Such was the question proposed to the Observatory of Cambridge. There was no lack of funds; the difficulty was purely constructional.

After considerable discussion as to the best form and principle of the proposed instrument the work was finally commenced. According to the calculations of the Observatory of Cambridge, the tube of the new reflector would require to be 280 feet in length, and the object-glass sixteen feet in diameter.

Regarding the choice of locality, that matter was promptly settled. The object was to select some lofty mountain, and there are not many of these in the United States.

In fact there are but two chains of moderate elevation, between which runs the magnificent Mississippi, the "king of rivers," as these Republican Yankees delight to call it.

Eastwards rise the Appalachians, the very highest point of which, in New Hampshire, does not exceed the very moderate altitude of 5,600 feet.

On the west, however, rise the Rocky Mountains, that immense range which runs up the whole of North America. The highest elevation of this range does not exceed 10,700 feet. With this elevation, nevertheless, the Gun Club had to be content, inasmuch as they had determined that both telescope and Columbiad should be erected within the limits of the Union. All the necessary apparatus was consequently sent on to the summit of Long's Peak, in the territory of Missouri.

Neither pen nor language can describe the multifarious difficulties which the American engineers had to surmount, or the prodigies of daring and skill which they accomplished. They had to raise enormous stones, massive pieces of wrought iron, heavy corner-clamps and huge portions of cylinder, with an object-glass weighing nearly 30,000 lb., above the line of perpetual snow for more than 10,000 feet in height, after crossing desert prairies, impenetrable forests, fearful rapids, far from all centres of population, and in the midst of savage regions, in which every detail of life becomes an almost insoluble problem. And yet, notwithstanding these innumerable obstacles, American genius triumphed. In less than a year, towards the close of September, the gigantic reflector rose into the air to a height of 280 feet. It was raised by means of an enormous iron crane; an ingenious mechanism allowed it to be easily adjusted, and to follow the stars from the one horizon to the other during their journey through the heavens.

It had cost 400,000 dollars. The first time it was directed towards the moon, the observers evinced both curiosity and anxiety. What were they about to discover in the field of this telescope which magnified objects 48,000 times? Would they perceive peoples, herds of lunar animals, towns, lakes, seas? No! there was nothing which science had not already discovered! and the volcanic nature of the moon was everywhere verified.

But the telescope of the Rocky Mountain, before doing its duty to the Gun Club, rendered immense services to astronomy. Thanks to its power, the depths of the heavens were sounded to the utmost extent; the apparent diameter of a great number of stars was accurately measured; and Mr. Clark, of the Cambridge staff, resolved the Crab nebula in Taurus, which the giant reflector of Lord Rosse had never been able to decompose.

## CHAPTER 24

# FINAL DETAILS

It was the 22nd November; the departure was to take place in ten days. One operation alone remained to be accomplished to bring all to a happy conclusion, an operation delicate and perilous, requiring infinite precautions, and against the success of which Captain Nicholl had laid his third bet. It was, in fact, nothing less than the loading of the Columbiad with 400,000 pounds of gun-cotton. Nicholl had thought, perhaps not without reason, that the handling of such formidable quantities of pyroxyle would, in all probability, involve a grave catastrophe; and that this immense mass of eminently inflammable matter would inevitably ignite under the pressure of the projectile.

There were indeed dangers arising as before from the carelessness of the Americans, but Barbicane had set his heart on success, and took all possible precautions. In the first place, he was very careful as to the transport of the gun-cotton to Stones Hill. He had it conveyed in small quantities, carefully packed in sealed cases. These were brought by rail from Tampa Town to the camp, and thence were taken to the Columbiad by barefooted workmen, who deposited them in their places by cranes placed at the mouth of the cannon. No steam-engine was permitted to work, and every fire was extinguished within two miles of the gun.

Even in November they feared to work by day, lest the sun's rays falling on the gun-cotton might lead to unhappy results. This led to their working at night, by light produced in a vacuum by means of Rühmkorff's apparatus, which threw an artificial brightness into the depths of the Columbiad. There the cartridges were arranged with the utmost regularity, and wired so as to transmit to all of them simultaneously the electric spark by which this mass of gun-cotton was to be ignited.

By the 28th November, 800 cartridges had been placed

in the bottom of the Columbiad. So far the operation had been successful! But what confusion, what anxieties, what struggles were undergone by President Barbicane! In vain had he refused admission to Stones Hill; every day the inquisitive neighbours scaled the palisades, some even carrying their imprudence to the point of smoking while surrounded by bales of gun-cotton. Barbicane was in a perpetual state of alarm.

J. T. Maston seconded him to the best of his ability, by giving vigorous chase to the intruders, and carefully picking up the lighted cigar ends which the Yankees threw about. A somewhat difficult task; seeing that more than 300,000 persons were gathered round the enclosure. Michel Ardan had volunteered to superintend the transport of the cartridges to the mouth of the Columbiad; but the president, having surprised him with an enormous cigar in his mouth, while he was hunting out the rash spectators to whom he himself offered so dangerous an example, saw that he could not trust this fearless smoker, and was therefore obliged to mount a special guard over him.

At last, Providence being propitious, this wonderful loading came to a happy termination, Captain Nicholl's third bet thus being lost. It remained now to introduce the projectile into the Columbiad, and to place it on its soft bed of gun-cotton.

But before doing this, all those things necessary for the journey had to be carefully arranged in the projectile. These were numerous; and had Ardan been allowed to follow his own wishes, there would have been no space remaining for the travellers. It is impossible to conceive of half the things this charming Frenchman wished to convey to the moon. A veritable stock of useless trifles! But Barbicane interfered and refused anything not absolutely needed. Several thermometers, barometers, and telescopes were packed in the instrument case.

The travellers anxious to survey the moon carefully during their voyage, took to facilitate their studies, Bœr and Moëller's excellent *Mappa Selenographica,* a masterpiece of patience and observation, which they hoped would enable them to identify those physical features in the moon which they might see. This map reproduced with scrupulous

fidelity the smallest details of the lunar surface which faces
the earth; the mountains, valleys, craters, peaks, and ridges
were all represented, with their exact dimensions, relative
positions, and names; from the mountains Doërfel and Leib-
nitz on the eastern side of the disc, to the *Mare frigoris* of
the North Pole.

They took also three rifles and three fowling-pieces, and
a large quantity of bullets, shot, and powder.

"We cannot tell whom we shall have to deal with," said
Michel Ardan. "Men or beasts may possibly object to our
visit. It is only wise to take all precautions."

These defensive weapons were accompanied by pickaxes,
crow-bars, saws, and other useful implements, not to mention clothing adapted to every temperature, from that of
the polar regions to that of the torrid zone.

Ardan wished to convey a number of animals of different
sorts—not indeed a pair of every known species, as he could
not see the necessity of acclimatizing serpents, tigers, alligators, or any other noxious beasts in the moon. "Nevertheless," he said to Barbicane, "such useful beasts as bullocks,
cows, horses, and donkeys, would bear the journey very
well, and would also be very useful to us."

"I dare say, my dear Ardan," replied the president, "but
our projectile is no Noah's ark, from which it differs both
in dimensions and object. Let us confine ourselves to possi-
bilities."

After a prolonged discussion, it was agreed that the travellers should restrict themselves to a sporting-dog belonging
to Nicholl, and to a large Newfoundland. Several packets of
seeds were also included. Michel Ardan, indeed, was anxious to add some sacks full of earth to sow them in; as it
was, he took a dozen shrubs carefully wrapped up in straw
to plant in the moon.

The important question of provisions still remained, it
being necessary to provide against the possibility of their
finding the moon absolutely barren. Barbicane managed
so successfully that he supplied them with sufficient rations
for a year. These consisted of preserved meats and vegeta-
bles, reduced by strong hydraulic pressure to the smallest
possible dimensions. They were also supplied with brandy,
and took water enough for two months, being confident,

from astronomical observations, that there was no lack of moisture on the moon's surface. As to provisions, doubtless the inhabitants of the earth would find nourishment somewhere in the moon. Ardan never questioned this; indeed, had he done so, he would never have undertaken the journey.

"Besides," he said one day to his friends, "we shall not be completely abandoned by our terrestrial friends; they will take care not to forget us."

"No, indeed!" replied J. T. Maston.

"What do you mean?" asked Nicholl.

"Nothing would be simpler," replied Ardan; "the Columbiad will always be there. Well! whenever the moon is in the zenith, if not in perigee, that is about once a year, could you not send us a shell packed with provisions, which we might expect on some appointed day?"

"Hurrah! hurrah!" cried J. T. Maston; "what an ingenious fellow! what a splendid idea! Indeed, my good friends, we shall not forget you!"

"I shall count upon you! Then, you see, we shall receive news regularly from the earth, and we shall indeed be stupid if we hit upon no plan for communicating with our good friends here!"

These words inspired such confidence that Michel Ardan carried all the Gun Club with him in his enthusiasm. What he said seemed so simple and so easy, so sure of success, that none could be so sordidly attached to this earth as to hesitate to follow the three travellers on their lunar expedition.

All at last being ready it remained to place the projectile in the Columbiad, an operation abundantly involving dangers and difficulties.

The enormous shell was conveyed to the summit of Stones Hill. There, powerful cranes raised it, and held it suspended over the mouth of the cylinder.

It was a fearful moment! What if the chains should break under its enormous weight? The sudden fall of such a body would inevitably cause the gun-cotton to explode!

Fortunately this did not happen; and some hours later the projectile descended gently into the heart of the cannon and rested on its couch of pyroxyle, a veritable bed of ex-

plosive eider-down. Its pressure had no result other than
the more effectual ramming down of the charge of the Columbiad.

"I have lost," said the Captain, who forthwith paid President Barbicane the sum of 3,000 dollars.

Barbicane did not wish to accept the money from one
of his fellow-travellers, but gave way at last before the de-
termination of Nicholl, who wished to fulfil all his engage-
ments before leaving the earth.

"Now," said Michel Ardan, "I have only one thing more
to wish for you, my brave Captain."

"What is that?" asked Nicholl.

"It is that you may lose your two other bets! Then we
shall be sure not to be stopped on our journey!"

## CHAPTER 25

# FIRE!

The 1st December had arrived! the fatal day! for, if the projectile were not fired that very night at 10h. 46m. 40s. p.m., more than eighteen years must roll by before the moon would again present herself under the same conditions of zenith and perigee.

The weather was magnificent. Despite the approach of winter, the sun shone brightly, and bathed in its radiant light that earth which three of its denizens were about to abandon for a new world.

How many persons lost their rest on the night which preceded this long-expected day! All hearts beat with disquietude, save only the heart of Michel Ardan. That imperturbable personage came and went with his habitual business-like air, while nothing whatever indicated that any unusual matter preoccupied his mind.

After dawn, an innumerable multitude covered the prairie which extends, as far as the eye can reach, round Stones Hill. Every quarter of an hour the railway brought fresh accessions of sightseers; and, according to the statement of the *Tampa Town Observer*, not less than five million spectators thronged the soil of Florida.

For a whole month previously, the mass of these persons had bivouacked round the enclosure, and laid the foundations for what was afterwards called "Ardan's Town." The whole plain was covered with huts, cottages, and tents. Every nation under the sun was represented there; and every language might be heard spoken at once. It was a perfect Babel re-enacted.

All the various classes of American society mingled together in terms of absolute equality. Bankers, farmers, sailors, cotton-planters, brokers, merchants, watermen, magistrates, elbowed each other in the most free-and-easy way. Louisiana Creoles fraternized with farmers from Indiana;

Kentucky and Tennessee gentlemen and haughty Virginians conversed with trappers and the half-savages of the lakes and butchers from Cincinnati.

Broad-brimmed white hats and Panamas, blue cotton trousers, light coloured stockings, cambric frills, were all displayed; while upon shirt-fronts, wristbands, and neckties, upon every finger, even upon the very *ears*, they wore an assortment of rings, shirt-pins, brooches, and trinkets, whose value was equalled only by their execrable taste. Women, children, and servants, in equally expensive dress, surrounding their husbands, fathers, or masters, who resembled the patriarchs of tribes in the midst of their immense households.

At mealtimes, all fell to work upon the dishes peculiar to the Southern States, and consumed, with an appetite that threatened speedy exhaustion of the victualling powers of Florida, fricasseed frog, stuffed monkey, fish chowder, underdone 'possum, and racoon steak. And as for the liquors which accompanied this indigestible repast! The shouts, the vociferations that resounded through the bars and taverns decorated with glasses, tankards, and bottles of marvellous shape, mortars for pounding sugar, and bundles of straws! "Mint-julep!" roars one of the barmen; "Claret sangaree!" shouts another; "Cocktail!" "Brandy-smash!" "Real mint-julep in the new style!" All these cries intermingled to produce a bewildering and deafening hubbub.

But on this day, 1st December, such sounds were rare. No one thought of eating or drinking, and at four p.m. there were vast numbers of spectators who had not even taken their customary lunch! And, a still more significant fact, even the national passion for gambling seemed quelled for the time under the general excitement of the hour.

Up till nightfall, a dull, noiseless agitation, such as precedes great catastrophes, ran through the anxious multitude. An indescribable uneasiness pervaded all minds, an indefinable sensation which oppressed the heart. Everyone wished it were over.

However, about seven o'clock, the heavy silence was dissipated. The moon rose above the horizon. Millions of hurrahs hailed her appearance. She was punctual to the rendezvous, and shouts of welcome greeted her on all sides, as her pale beams shone gracefully in the clear heavens.

At this moment the three intrepid travellers appeared. This was the signal for renewed cries of still greater intensity. Instantly the vast assemblage, as with one accord, struck up the national hymn of the United States, and "Yankee Doodle," sung by five million of hearty throats, rose like a roaring tempest to the fairest limits of the atmosphere. Then a profound silence reigned throughout the crowd.

The Frenchman and the two Americans had by this time entered the reserved enclosure in the centre of the multitude. They were accompanied by the members of the Gun Club, and by deputations sent from all the European Observatories. Barbicane, cool and collected, was giving his final directions: Nicholl, with compressed lips, his arms crossed behind his back, walked with a firm and measured step. Michel Ardan, always easy, dressed in thorough traveller's costume, leathern gaiters on his legs, pouch by his side, in loose velvet suit, cigar in mouth, was full of inexhaustible gaiety, laughing, joking, playing pranks with J. T. Maston. In one word, he was the thorough "Frenchman" (and worse, a "Parisian") to the last moment.

Ten o'clock struck; the moment had arrived for taking their places in the projectile! The necessary operations for the descent, and the subsequent removal of the cranes and scaffolding over the mouth of the Columbiad, would still take a little time.

Barbicane had regulated his chronometer to the tenth part of a second by that of Murchison the engineer, who was given the duty of firing the gun by an electric spark. Thus the travellers within the projectile were able to follow with their eyes the impassive seconds' hand which marked the precise moment of their departure.

The moment had arrived for saying "Good-bye!" The scene was moving. Despite his feverish gaiety, even Michel Ardan was touched. J. T. Maston had found in his own dry eyes one ancient tear, which he had doubtless reserved for the occasion. He dropped it on the forehead of his dear president.

"Can I not go?" he said, "there is still time!"

"Impossible, old fellow!" replied Barbicane. A few moments later, the three fellow-travellers had ensconced themselves in the projectile, and screwed down the plate which covered the entrance-aperture. The mouth of the Columbiad, now completely uncovered, was open to the sky.

The moon advanced upwards in a heaven of the purest clearness, outshining in her passage the twinkling light of the stars. She passed over the constellation of the Twins, and was now nearing the half-way point between the horizon and the zenith. A terrible silence weighed upon the entire scene! Not a breath of wind upon the earth! not a sound of breathing from the countless chests of the spectators! Their hearts seemed afraid to beat! All eyes were fixed upon the yawning mouth of the Columbiad.

Murchison followed with his eye the hand of his chronometer. It wanted scarce forty seconds to the moment of departure, but each second seemed to last an age! At the twentieth there was a general shudder, as it occurred to the minds of that vast assemblance that the bold travellers shut up within the projectile were also counting those terrible seconds. Some few cries here and there escaped the crowd.

"Thirty-five!—thirty-six!—thirty-seven!—thirty-eight!—thirty-nine!—forty! FIRE! ! !"

Instantly Murchison pressed with his finger the key of the electric battery, completed the circuit, and released the spark into the breach of the Columbiad.

An appalling, unearthly report followed instantly, such as can be compared to nothing whatever, not even to the roar of thunder or the blast of volcanic explosions! No words can convey the slightest idea of the terrific sound! An immense spout of fire shot up from the bowels of the earth as from a crater. The earth heaved, and with great difficulty a few spectators obtained a momentary glimpse of the projectile victoriously cleaving the air in the midst of the fiery vapours!

## CHAPTER 26

# FOUL WEATHER

At the moment when that pyramid of fire rose to a prodigious height into the air the glare of the flame lit up the whole of Florida; and for a moment day superseded night over a vast expanse of the country. This immense canopy of fire was perceived at a distance of 100 miles out at sea, and more than one ship's captain entered in his log the appearance of this gigantic meteor.

The discharge of the Columbiad was accompanied by an earthquake. Florida was shaken to its very depths. The gases from the gun-cotton, expanded by heat, forced the atmosphere back with tremendous violence, and this artificial hurricane rushed like a waterspout through the air.

Not a single spectator remained on his feet: Men, women, children, all lay prostrate like ears of corn under a tempest. There ensued a terrible tumult; many of the people were seriously injured. J. T. Maston, who, despite of all dictates of prudence had kept ahead of the mass, was pitched back 120 feet, shooting like a projectile over the heads of his fellow-citizens. Three hundred thousand persons remained deaf for a time, and were as though struck stupefied.

As soon as the first effects were over, the injured, the deaf, and lastly, the crowd in general, woke up with frenzied cries. "Hurrah for Ardan! Hurrah for Barbicane! Hurrah for Nicholl!" rose to the skies. Thousands of persons, noses in the air, armed with telescopes and race-glasses, were questioning space, forgetting all contusions and emotions in the one idea of watching for the projectile. They looked in vain! It was no longer to be seen, and they were obliged to wait for telegrams from Long's Peak. The Director of the Cambridge Observatory was at his post on the Rocky Mountains; and to him, as a skilful and persevering astronomer, all observation had been entrusted.

But an unforeseen phenomenon came in to subject the public impatience to a severe trial.

The weather, hitherto so fine, suddenly changed; the sky

became heavy with clouds. It could not have been otherwise after the terrible derangement of the air, and the dispersion of the enormous quantity of vapour arising from the combustion of 200,000 lb. of pyroxyle!

On the morrow the horizon was covered with clouds—a thick and impenetrable curtain between earth and sky, which unhappily extended as far as the Rocky Mountains. It was a calamity! But since man had chosen so to disturb the atmosphere, he was bound to accept the consequences of his experiment.

Supposing, now, that the experiment had succeeded, the travellers having started on the 1st December, at 10h. 46m. 40s. p.m., were due at their destination on the 4th at midnight! So up to that time it would after all have been very difficult to observe, under such conditions, a body so small as the shell. Therefore they waited with what patience they might.

From the 4th to the 6th December inclusive, the weather remaining much the same in America, the great European instruments were constantly directed towards the moon, for the weather was there magnificent; but the comparative weakness of their telescopes prevented any trustworthy observations from being made.

On the 7th the sky seemed to lighten. They were in hope now, but their hope was of but short duration, and at night thick clouds again hid the starry vault from all eyes.

Matters were now becoming serious, when on the 9th, the sun reappeared for an instant, as if for the purpose of teasing the Americans. It was received with hisses; and wounded, no doubt, by such a reception, showed itself very sparing of its rays.

On the 10th, no change! J. T. Maston nearly went mad, and great fears were entertained regarding the brain of this worthy individual, hitherto so well preserved within his gutta-percha cranium.

But on the 11th one of those inexplicable tempests peculiar to those intertropical regions was let loose in the atmosphere. A terrific east wind swept away the groups of clouds which had been so long gathering, and at night the semi-disc of the orb of night rode majestically amidst the soft constellations of the sky.

## CHAPTER 27

# A NEW STAR

That very night, the startling news so impatiently awaited burst like a thunderbolt over the United States and thence, darting across the ocean, ran through all the telegraphic wires of the globe. Thanks to the gigantic reflector of Long's Peak the projectile had been detected. Here is the note received by the Director of the Observatory of Cambridge. It contains the scientific conclusion regarding this great experiment of the Gun Club.

"LONG'S PEAK, 12*th December*

"To the Officers of the Observatory of Cambridge.

"The projectile discharged by the Columbiad at Stones Hill has been detected by Messrs. Belfast and J. T. Maston, 12th December, at 8.47 p.m., the moon having entered her last quarter. This projectile has not arrived at its destination. It has passed to one side; but sufficiently near to be retained by the lunar attraction.

"The rectilinear movement has thus become changed into a circular motion of extreme velocity, and it is now pursuing an elliptical orbit round the moon, of which it has become a true satellite.

"The elements of this new star we have as yet been unable to determine; we do not yet know its velocity. This distance which separates it from the surface of the moon may be estimated at about 2,833 miles.

"However, two hypotheses come here into our consideration.

"1. Either the attraction of the moon will end by drawing them into itself, and the travellers will attain their destination; or:

"2. The projectile, following an immutable law, will continue to gravitate round the moon till the end of time.

"At some future time, our observations will be able to decide this, but till then the experiment of the Gun Club can have no other result than to have provided our solar system with a new star.

"J. BELFAST."

To how many questions did this unexpected denouement give rise? What mysterious results was the future reserving for the investigations of science? At all events, the names of Nicholl, Barbicane, and Michel Ardan were certain to be immortalized in the annals of astronomy!

When the despatch from Long's Peak had once become known, there was but one universal feeling of surprise and alarm. Was it possible to go to the aid of these bold travellers? No! for they had placed themselves beyond the pale of humanity, by crossing the limits imposed by the Creator on his earthly creatures. They had air enough for *two* months; they had victuals enough for *twelve; but after that*? There was only one man who would not admit that the situation was desperate—he alone had confidence; and that was their devoted friend J. T. Maston.

He never let them get out of sight. His home was henceforth the post at Long's Peak; his horizon, the mirror of that immense reflector. As soon as the moon rose above the horizon, he immediately caught her in the field of the telescope; he never let her go for an instant out of his sight, and followed her assiduously in her course through the stellar spaces. He watched with untiring patience the passage of the projectile across her silvery disc, and so the worthy man remained in perpetual communication with his three friends, whom he did not despair of seeing again some day.

"Those three men," said he, "have carried into space all the resources of art, science, and industry. With that, one can do anything; and you will see that, some day, they will come out all right."